Avra Wing writes with
an original voice to savor and enjoy...
and creates an offbeat,
irresistible heroine to love

Angie, I Says

"Readers who enjoyed Cher in *Moonstruck* will also take a liking to Tina Scacciapensieri... with a good dose of humor, this heroine entertains."
—*Booklist*

•

"Highly original... written in an insanely lyrical, fast-paced style."
—*Pittsburgh Press*

•

"Avra Wing is a gifted writer, indeed... to tell a story that is so graceful and touching."
—**Elinor Lipman, author of *Then She Found Me***

•

"Appealing... [with] unusual brio... Wing illuminates the family dynamic as well as the emotions that bind people to their friends, lovers, and co-workers."
—*Publishers Weekly*

•

"A plucky, tender-hearted first novel... Avra Wing's heroine is an original."
—**Elizabeth Benedict, author of *Slow Dancing* and *The Beginner's Book of Dreams***

•

"Wing's strength is her observation of the tooth-and-claw infighting of family life; clearly she has talent... school of J. D. Salinger, all the way."

"Avra Wing is a natu
on the pulse of the t
honest novel. She is
—**Sarah Gilbert, au

•

"An offbeat love story...winning raves!"

—*Library Journal*

"Perceptive and witty.... Tina Scacciapensieri has a voice not quickly forgotten."

—*Erie Time-News*

•

"Tina is a strong-voiced sage who speaks simply, but insightfully, about the conflicts, failures and triumphs of human relationships."

—*Newport News, Virginia*

ATTENTION: SCHOOLS AND CORPORATIONS

WARNER books are available at quantity discounts with bulk purchase for educational, business, or sales promotional use. For information, please write to: SPECIAL SALES DEPARTMENT, WARNER BOOKS, 1271 AVENUE OF THE AMERICAS, NEW YORK, N.Y. 10020.

**ARE THERE WARNER BOOKS
YOU WANT BUT CANNOT FIND IN YOUR LOCAL STORES?**

You can get any WARNER BOOKS title in print. Simply send title and retail price, plus 95¢ per order and 95¢ per copy to cover mailing and handling costs for each book desired. New York State and California residents add applicable sales tax. Enclose check or money order only, no cash please, to: WARNER BOOKS, P.O. BOX 690, NEW YORK, N.Y. 10019.

Angie, I Says

Avra Wing

WARNER BOOKS

A Time Warner Company

If you purchase this book without a cover you should be aware that this book may have been stolen property and reported as "unsold and destroyed" to the publisher. In such case neither the author nor the publisher has received any payment for this "stripped book."

Grateful acknowledgment is made to Nancy A. Silber for permission to reprint lyrics from "Be Happy Now."

WARNER BOOKS EDITION

Copyright © 1991 by Avra Wing
All rights reserved.

Cover Design by Anne Twomey
Cover Photography by Ryszard Horowitz

Warner Books, Inc.
1271 Avenue of the Americas
New York, N.Y. 10020

 A Time Warner Company

Printed in the United States of America

Originally published in hardcover by Warner Books.
First Printed in Paperback: August, 1992

10 9 8 7 6 5 4 3 2

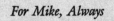

For Mike, Always

I would like to thank my agent, Jean Naggar, for believing in the book, and my editors, Leslie Keenan and Jamie Raab. I am also extremely grateful to Dr. Frances Cohen for her invaluable support. I want to thank, too, Dr. Robert Carroll for his help, and Jean Downer for her loving attention to my child, which gave me the chance to write. And to Alex and Eli, thanks for more than I can say.

Part
I

Chapter 1

Can I get that file for you after lunch?" I'm in the Ladies, in the stall next to Angie.

"Sure, no problem, Tina," she tells me. "Lazy bitch."

I crack up. I mean, I would of wet my pants except I'd already just gone. "Angie, you're too much."

"Yeah," she says, coming out. "Too much here, and too much here." She points to her breasts and backside.

I have to laugh again. "Naw. That's what's gonna get you boyfriends."

"Oh, listen to her," she says to Rochelle. "What do you know about it, Princess Di? She thinks the guys wanna go out with her 'cause she types good. Don't you? Yeah, you think Marv's always hanging over you 'cause you know how to use the Selectric."

"Come on, Angie," Rochelle butts in, "she ain't as dumb as she looks."

I let it pass. I'm in a hurry. But Ange gives her a dirty look.

Ange is my best friend at the office. Me and Tony are friends, too, but he's a guy so it don't count. If it wasn't for them, though, I would of quit a long time ago, believe me. This place isn't so great. I mean, the pay is just so-so and it's not like it's a real newspaper or anything. Just a fucking trade for some guys think they're such hot shit 'cause they make computers and like that. *The MicroCircuit.* I mean, you tell people where you work, they never heard of it. Then they're always giving us this crap about how we're a team and how special we all are and all that. Makes me wanna puke. When they start in with that shit, Angie and me look at each other cross-eyed. It gets me pissed, let me tell you.

But it don't bother Angie, not really. She likes the place. She must—she's been here twelve years. Can you believe it? I would never stay anywhere so long. I'm coming up on three years now and I can't take much more. But Angie's no quitter. How else did she stay with that bastard of a husband all this time?

I seen him, and believe me, he's nothing special. Short. A big belly. Maybe he was good-looking once. Maybe. I don't know what Ange sees in him. She was out for a week one time. She said it was flu, but I could tell. The scuzzball hit her and she was ashamed to come in with the marks on her. *He* had hit *her* and *she* was ashamed. That's how it is with some people.

But you can't talk to Ange about it. I mean, I tell her, "Leave the bastard. You're still pretty. The guys'll be all over you." But she says no. She raised three kids with him, she says. Like that's a reason. The kids are lucky they're alive, if you aks me, with that dirtbag for a father. The youngest is sixteen. Enough, I says. You don't need him no more. But she says, "What would he do without me?" What can you do when someone talks that way?

But today I got no time even for Ange. I got an appointment uptown. Fern, over in Editorial, gave me the name. I figure, I got the benefits, I can go to whoever I please. I don't need Dr. Crapanzano telling my business all over the neighborhood.

* * *

I know I'm gonna be late, especially if this dirtbag elevator don't come soon. And then I'll have to eat lunch at my desk, unless I grab a couple of franks outside. And then that bitch Frieda's gonna notice if I come in after two o'clock. Like it's any of her business.

Some people ain't happy unless they're making trouble. Problem with her, she thinks this stinking office is the whole goddamn world. She hasn't noticed people have other things to think about. I mean, she's pathetic, really. But I think if she actually ever got someone fired it would be the high point of her life.

She should of been in the army. Or a prison warden. No wonder they made her office manager. She don't let nothing get by.

So here's the elevator. Congratulations. I always like peeking at the other floors, seeing who gets on where. Some of these women, work upstairs on *Skirt*, dress like they're on the moon or something. And the guys. Forget about it. Real freaks.

It's the ones in suits I like. The good suits. You can tell. That's the kind of guy I wanna go out with. Not like the jerks I see. I mean, Vinnie's got a suit, but it's green.

I guess Vinnie's okay, though. It's not like he's like Angie's Jim or anything. Though I guess maybe I shouldn't talk. I mean, Angie has her problems, but at least she was married, or as good as married, before she got herself knocked up.

Chapter 2

Not that I'm positive or nothing. Just pretty sure. I mean, I haven't missed my friend once since I was twelve years old and came home for lunch with this brown crap in my panties. I thought I'd dirtied myself, I was so dumb. But my sister, Jeanette, set me straight: "No, you little dope," she says. "Now you're a woman."

I didn't feel no different. Like you're supposed to feel grown up all of a sudden. "Now you can have a baby," Jeanette tells me. Scared the shit out of me. I mean, I thought it could just happen, I was that stupid.

Just to be sure, I wouldn't let no guy come near me for a while after that. I kept thinking that maybe just looking at a guy too hard or something and I'd be pregnant. And I couldn't do it to Pop. I mean, he had enough problems raising us two girls. Finish school, finish school he was always telling me. He was afraid for me.

So I finished school. Big deal. Now I can work taking care of other people's shit. Fern says I should go to college, but I don't know. No one I know did that. Anyways, at least I'm not working at the ShopRite.

Jeanette talked big about going to college for a while.

She was going out with this college guy, but he dropped her, and after that we didn't hear nothing about no college. Then she married Nick, and had Donna, then Joey. Now she's not going nowhere.

The subways, boy, they're the pits, especially in the summer. I mean, they overheat them in the winter, but you're just glad to be down there, out of the cold. But the summer—you get into a car the air-conditioning's broken, you could die. I mean like hundreds of dirty, sweaty bodies, everybody in a bad mood. And garbage all over everywhere. Smells like rotten fruit. And that's on a good day.

Some people have money for cabs. Don't aks me how. I mean, it's over a buck just to put your backside on the seat. Really. You sit down, it's a buck fifteen. Plus tip.

I can see myself doing it someday, though. I'll have on this beautiful suit—real classy—and I'll be getting in a cab and going to Bergdorf Goodman's to buy some more stuff I don't need. Then I'll take a cab back home to Park Avenue. Right.

Maybe I'm not really pregnant. I mean, I always hear the girls say your body changes. Your period changes when you get older. I just turned thirty, if you can believe it. It could be nothing. But me and Vinnie got a little careless, so I think maybe this is it.

Sometimes on the train I play a game. I call it God's Grace. I pick out someone and pretend I'm them. Some fat middle-aged lady wearing knee-highs under her dress instead of panty hose, some old guy with his pants bunched up in a belt, they've gotten so big on him. A young guy, checking himself out in the reflection in the window, thinks he's really something. A tall blonde acting like she don't notice everyone's staring at her. Some man in a business suit pretending like he got on by mistake and like what is he doing here.

Then I think about what their lives are. Where they're going on the train, where they've come from. If they're married, have any friends. I don't know why I do it. It's fun, or something. I mean, I guess I should read the newspaper or something.

So I'm going to this fancy doctor. I'm not scared or nothing. Up here, they don't care if you're married or what. My money's as good as anybody's, even if I do live in Brooklyn.

I'm looking at this waiting room and I don't believe what I'm seeing. I mean, you sit here with all these smiling pregnant ladies, and all these magazines with cute kids all over the place, and these pictures of mothers with their babies on every wall, you better be happy. If someone was here because she couldn't have a baby, or let's say she wanted an abortion, or just lost a baby, I think she'd go crazy just walking into this place.

Fern says all gynecologists hate women, but that this guy ain't too bad. I guess. He seems sweet, like my uncle Louie. Like every woman's some big deal and he don't know what to say. Who knows why a guy decides to spend his life looking up into women and delivering babies. Maybe you're in a delivery room enough times it's almost like giving birth yourself.

He thinks I'm pregnant. He's smiling. Like it's so wonderful. He aks me how I feel. I feel like I'm gonna scream. Friggin' Vinnie. If he thinks I'm gonna stand up in public with him in that green suit and get married, he's nuts.

The goddamn nurse thinks it's great, too. Good. Everybody's real happy. I'm the one has to go home and break the news.

So here I am with all this crap about eating right stuck in my hand. Suddenly we're all concerned about the baby. It's two o'clock, I'm still on Seventy-eighth Street and have to be downtown now, and I should worry about a balanced diet. Like I'm gonna start drinking milk this minute. That bitch Frieda better not say word one.

Chapter 3

*L*uckily, when I get back the painters are there, and everybody's shifting around trying to find a place to work so no one notices when I walk in. Everyone's real put out about the mess. I mean, people are never happy. First they complain about how shitty the place looks, then someone gets around to painting or putting in new carpeting or something—and where they got that orange color from I'll never know, they sure didn't aks me what I thought—they complain they can't get no work done. I mean, there's Gene with a story for the early section screaming, "I'm on deadline!" to a bunch of guys couldn't care less. They gotta move his desk now, they tell him. That's what the boss said.

I dial Angie's extension.

"What the hell you calling for?" she says. "Your leg's broke? You can't walk two steps to my desk?"

"Don't give me a hard time, Ange. Can you meet me in the bathroom in five minutes?"

We have to wait until the Ladies is empty. Then finally I come out with it. Angie just shakes her head. "Sweet Jesus, Tina, I thought you was smarter than that."

"Thanks a lot, Ange," I says, and she sees I'm crying.

"Sorry, kid." She gives me a hug. "Look, Tina, it's early. You're not showing. No one has to know. You get married, you have a kid. No one's gonna say nothing."

I nod my head. I feel like the world's biggest idiot.

"What did Vinnie say?"

"He don't know."

"So you gonna tell him or wait for the christening?"

"Sure, I'm gonna tell him."

She don't like the way I says this. "It's his, ain't it?"

"Of course it's his."

"So?"

"So what?"

"So what's the problem?"

I'm leaning there against the sink looking down at the cracked tile. They've been promising us a new Ladies for two years now.

"Tina?"

"I don't know what the problem is. Maybe I don't wanna get married. Maybe I don't wanna marry Vinnie."

Now she really don't know what to say. "Vinnie's such a sweet guy, Teen. That time he came over I didn't have no water. Fixed me up and no charge. And he's crazy about you."

She can see I'm not listening. "Tina, if it's his kid, he's got a right."

The hell with that, I tell her. *I* got a right. A right to what? she says. To be on welfare?

She's angry. She's gonna really let me have it, but two girls from Payroll come in and Angie leaves.

Frieda's at my desk when I get back. "Is everything all right, Tina?" she aks like she'd be only too happy to hear I'm sick or something. She's spooky. It's like she's got X-ray vision or some shit like that. And no matter what you say, she acts like you're lying. She wouldn't believe Jesus himself if he worked here. I mean, she'd be looking over his shoulder to make sure he didn't cheat on the time chart.

Thing is, I know how to handle her. People like Frieda,

you gotta go them one better. "It's nothing, Frieda. I knew you'd notice, though, you're so considerate. I know you're busy so I won't keep you. But thanks for aksing about me."

See, she don't know what to say. The idea is to try to make her feel like a piece of shit 'cause she doubted you. So then maybe she'll stop sticking her nose in your business every minute. She'll go pick on somebody else.

Yeah, I'm smart all right. So how come I went and did a dumb thing like get myself pregnant? And I'm gonna have to tell Fern 'cause she's no dope and I know she's wondering what the hell I wanted the name of her doctor for. But I can trust her. She don't have a big mouth.

Angie don't like her, but Angie's wrong this time. You can't hate everybody went to college. And no matter how many times I tell Ange I'm half-Jewish, she forgets. Or says, "Yeah, but you're different." That gets me angry, but I don't say nothing. I guess with a name like Scacciapensieri people figure you're Italian or something.

I don't hate nobody. It's stupid. You can't live in this world, you hate too many people. Try riding the subway if you don't like Spanish or black people or the Chinese.

I mean, the only thing, I find it strange when a black person owns a dog. It don't seem right, somehow. But other than that, I figure everyone's more or less the same. I tell this to Ange, but she don't buy it. Some black girl gives her a nasty look, her skin crawls. Ignorant, she calls them. She can't stand it when we're going home on the train and these black kids get on yammering at each other. I figure they're kids, but Ange gets her back up. "You'd think they'd drop dead or something if they shut their traps for two seconds," she says.

It takes all kinds, Angie, I says. She says I should join the UN. I don't know. Maybe they got a good maternity plan.

Chapter 4

So it's the end of the day and now Ange is acting like she don't wanna talk to me. Just great. I never seen her like this, like she don't know what to do so she stays away. You think you know someone.

I go over to Fern to aks maybe she'd like to have a drink or something after work. I can tell she's surprised and a little worried. I mean, I know I'm not her usual type. For a friend, I mean. So I try to make it sound real casual, not too important. Then I says there's something I'd like to talk to her about. She's relieved because she sees it's just a one-time thing.

I'm not offended. I mean, what have we got in common? We like each other and all, but we don't hang out. But Fern's not a snob. I mean, some of these people, they think clerical's like having leprosy. They don't talk to us. They don't know nobody's name.

Anyways, Fern can't do it but makes a date for lunch tomorrow. It's funny, when you wanna do something real bad, tomorrow seems a long ways off. I remember as a kid I would go crazy if we was going to Coney Island or something and it rained and we had to wait. Ma would scream at me, "It's only a day, we'll go tomorrow." But I wouldn't listen. I had a fit. And Jeanette called me baby. Then I'd go after her.

So Fern tells me tomorrow and I feel like if I don't talk to somebody my head'll bust open. Tony aks me to go with the guys for drinks, but that's the last thing I need. I mean, maybe I could talk to him alone. Maybe. But I'm in no mood to be one of the boys. I go back for my coat and Ange is kind of hanging around my desk.

"Going to the subway?" she aks.

"Yeah, I guess. The limo broke down so I'm taking the train today."

She don't even smile. "Oh. I thought maybe you was going somewheres with Fern."

"Naw. Come on. And cheer up." Then I whisper, "Shit, I'm the one with the problem."

We leave the building, nodding to the maintenance guy like any other night, and she puts her hand on my arm.

"Please, Tina, it would be wrong to get rid of this baby."

I look at her like she's crazy, then turn my head around to see if maybe someone heard. We're walking down Forty-second, millions of people, but nobody cares what we got to say to each other.

"Ange, I didn't say nothing about getting rid of no baby."

"But you're thinking about it, Tina, I can tell. Why else would you be talking about not marrying Vinnie?"

"Maybe I just don't love him enough, Angie. Ain't that a good enough reason?"

She shakes her head. "Not now. Oh, Tina, what kind of life is it for a girl if she don't get married?"

I let out a breath. It's funny. Ange is the last person I thought would give me a hard time. "I didn't say I wasn't going to."

"Oh, Teen. Maybe it ain't the way you wanted, but it'll be nice. You'll be the prettiest bride."

"Ange, please, I don't know what I'm gonna do. I gotta think."

"But not about an abortion, please, Tina."

Now I'm mad. "Look, Ange, I don't believe in that sin shit, I'll tell you right off. I wasn't raised religious and you know it. I don't go to church and I'm not gonna have no priest tell me what I can and can't do. Let the pope have a baby he don't want and see how he likes it. He don't like abortion? Let him send money to all the girls with babies they can't afford to take care of."

"You shouldn't talk like that, Tina." She's real hurt and I feel bad.

"I'm sorry, Ange. Look, that stuff is fine for you, but I wasn't raised to be nothing and I can't start now. So let's not get into it 'cause we'll just have a fight."

She shakes her head. "I ain't preaching nothing. I'm just saying a baby is something very special and you gotta realize that. No two babies are the same. You get rid of this baby, that's it. Who knows? This baby could be the most special baby of all time, and no one would ever know."

We're almost to the station. "Ange, please, don't do this to me now. Look, I don't have nothing against babies. I like babies. I like kids. But I have to think about what I wanna do."

Ange looks at me hard. "You got a nice guy like Vinnie wants to marry you and you don't even care. You'd rather kill this baby. I can't understand you, Tina."

I feel like she's poured ice water into my heart. I mean, I can hardly get my breath. People are bumping into us, rushing every which way. I can't move, I'm just staring at her.

"Angie, please."

She looks like she's gonna cry. "Listen, I'll talk to you tomorrow. I gotta go. You coming?"

I shake my head. I don't know what I wanna do. She gives me another look, then leaves. I'm standing there like a prize idiot. Half the people in the city trying to get home pushing around me. I turn and start walking. I don't know where I'm going, but I'm moving.

Chapter 5

In New York, everybody walks fast. Everybody's going someplace, and going there in a hurry. I must be the only one in the whole goddamn city don't know where she's headed.

I gotta decide. It's funny, I always think New York's got its own set of directions. You know. Uptown and downtown instead of north and south. Anyways, I don't know what I'm in the mood for. I go in for a drink, some guy'll come over and hit on me. Some jerk. The last thing I need. Maybe shopping. Macy's. To buy what? I aks myself. Maternity clothes?

And no go on that drink, anyways. I mean, it's bad for the baby, right? You can't see my belly or nothing yet. But this thing, this person, whatever, is taking over.

So I keep walking uptown, thinking. Don't aks me why I'm going uptown, unless I wanna be headed as far away from Brooklyn as possible. Then I'm having this funny thought like I'm gonna run into the doctor and he'll tell me it was a mistake. Fat chance. Maybe I'm thinking if I walk fast or something the baby'll shake loose.

That happens, don't it? I mean, you can lose a baby. I

know lots of girls it happened to. Then I'd be back at square one.

I head west to Madison. Third Avenue's boring. Nothing interesting to look at. The stores all have the same clothes and all the buildings are new. Madison has all those small, fancy places with foreign names, one after the other. Clothes, handbags, shoes so beautiful they're like little statues, jewelry, makeup, chocolate.

It would be fun, I guess, to show a kid this place. "Oh look at that window, honey, isn't that beautiful?" Jesus. A baby. Who the hell am I to have a kid? Well, I guess that never stopped no one. I mean, if everyone was to grow up when they had children, it'd solve a lot of problems.

I guess I'd be an okay mother. I mean, I know I would love the kid. Who could help it? You see people with their kids sometimes, you can't believe it. Like the women are always yelling at them. The women yell, the guys tease them, especially the boys. Like they don't know how else to talk to them. Like the kids are little idiots or something put there for their amusement. And that's in the normal families. Someone hurts a kid, they should be put away forever. That I just can't understand.

I get a kick out of these ladies with the sneakers on. Look at 'em. Some of them are lady execs in nice suits, must of cost two hundred at least, leather briefcases, and these cloddy Nikes with sweat socks. Like they don't care what they look like. Or like they're such big athletes they have to throw on their track shoes the second they hit the street.

And now some of the secy's are doing it too, like the little sisters trying to look grown up by wearing their big sisters' clothes. But some of 'em, Jesus, they're still trying to put one foot in front of the other in their high heels. Wobbling, like they're on stilts. I tell the girls at work, you look like you're trying out for the circus in that outfit. That don't go over too big.

They think I'm nuts for just wearing flats. But you can't move in them heels. You totter around like somebody's

Chinese wife. Some of 'em, with their heels and slit skirts, they might as well head straight for Eighth Avenue and walk the street. Of course, I don't say that to their faces.

It's funny how everybody gets a different idea about what's beautiful. I mean, to one person it's a black suit and to another it's a shiny, electric-blue dress. You go shopping, you say, Oh, that's an Angie dress, or, That's something only Frieda would wear. Or like those women who get stuck in the way they dressed ten, twenty years ago. You see 'em around. Hair teased like it's still the fifties, or little white gloves and a hat.

I'm moving and I don't have to think too hard. Maybe I should take up jogging. Then I wouldn't have to think at all.

Seventy-second. I'm getting tired. Things aren't so crazy here. Not too many offices. Just more of them pretty stores where you go in and say, "I'm looking for something in gray, Marie. You know what I like." And you sit down and they bring the stuff to you. What a hoot.

Chapter 6

Here's some people hanging out. What's this? A museum. I mean, not my usual, but tonight it seems like a good idea. Nobody I know's gonna be in there, and I don't feel like seeing nobody I know.

I mean, I'm not even sure what you're supposed to do in here, but it could work out. Maybe the baby'll get something out of this. Culture or something like that.

It's quiet here. Nobody's talking and that's okay by me. And it's even free tonight and that's a good thing, too, because the three-dollar admission is a rip-off if you aks me.

These pictures aren't so hard. You can see people in them and everything. But they're kind of sad, like everyone's alone. Everybody staring out a window at nothing, like Ma does when she's bad. Just sitting and staring like she's waiting for something to happen.

Maybe the guy who painted them was sick like that. Couldn't go nowhere. And he painted these. Ladies, men. Even two people they're in the same room, they got nothing to say to each other.

There's one picture here looks like my neighborhood. Feels like it, too. Rows of red brick houses. It's funny to see it up there like that. I'm wondering maybe the artist came from Brooklyn and changed his name or something.

Now what is with that guy over there? Did he come in to look at the pictures or at me? I hope he's getting an eyeful. I don't know, maybe he can tell I'm pregnant. Some people have a sixth sense about stuff like that.

I'm looking at him out of the corner of my eye just to check him out. What's the harm? But I'm telling myself to forget about it. I mean, now's not exactly the time. My life's enough of a mess.

I can't shake this jerk. I mean, he ain't bad looking. Nice suit, looks like he just came from work. A little old, maybe. I can't tell. Although nothing's wrong with an older guy. More settled. I mean, he's not forty or nothing.

Jeez, this is spooky. I go to a different room, two seconds later this guy just happens to be there. What is this, a game? I mean, if he's shy, he shouldn't be staring at girls in the goddamn museum. Makes me feel like my bra strap's showing or something.

I can't look at nothing now. That's how it is with guys. You try to do something, and some man comes along and wants you to pay attention to him. Then whatever it is you wanted is all over. I mean, some girls, they never wanna do nothing except have some guy interrupt them. Like their life's a big long nothing until a man taps them on the shoulder. Big deal. Then it's still a big long nothing, except you have to take his crap. But they never learn. You'd think their mothers were so happy or something. Some people can't take a hint.

"You following me?" I shocked him all right. But I figure, either I wait all night for him to talk to me, or I leave, which I'm not about to do, or I shake the guy up.

He smiles. Real sweet. Shit, he's cute. "Sorry. I guess I was. I couldn't help it. I just liked the way you were looking at the paintings. I didn't want to bother you. But I'm glad you said something."

So now it's my move and I don't know what to say. Being picked up is so sleazy, but he seems okay. Then I think about maybe he's some maniac gonna cut me or has some disease or something. I can't help it. You read the *Post* headlines, you can't help being scared.

"Well, could you stop staring at me? I mean, I came in to look around and stuff."

He smiles some more. He thinks I'm stupid. Good. Then he'll leave me alone.

"Ah, look. My name is Noah. What's yours?"

I tell him. It don't cost nothing.

"That's pretty. Do you work around here?"

"Maybe."

"Ah, you like Hopper?"

"Who?"

"Hopper, the artist." He points to the walls.

Now I really feel like a jerk.

"I don't know. Yeah, I guess I do." I'm moving away.

"Wait." He reaches into his pocket. "Here's my card." He hands it to me. NOAH LIEB, it says, ATTORNEY, and then the name of his company. I can't help but smile. I mean, I'm impressed.

"Just hold on to it, okay? Maybe we could have lunch sometime?"

"I don't know. I don't know if you're for real."

"What do you mean?"

"I mean anybody could get a card printed up." I wanna show him I'm not a little dummy gets all hot just 'cause a guy's a professional.

"Hey, you're tough."

And funniest thing. I feel like I'm gonna cry. I just wanna sit down and cry my eyes out. And I don't care who sees me. I'll cry in front of those pictures. Those people in them—they'll understand.

He's looking at me. He sees something. Like he's reading my mind. And I know I like him. You either like somebody or you don't. And that's all there is to it. I mean, Ange always kids me about Tony, but it ain't like that with us. Besides, I happen to know he's got the hots for Fern, but she won't give him the time of day. I mean, he ain't much to look at, but he's a nice guy. A smart guy. I don't know. Maybe if he dressed better.

You just can't make sense out of any of it. Somebody says: Why don't you like so-and-so? He's just your type. Whatever. It don't matter. Something don't click, forget about it.

So I tell him I'm a secretary for a major publishing company—like they do on the game shows not to give a plug to no one. What's it gonna hurt? The guy likes the way I look, I should be angry?

"Ah, Tina," he says, all uncomfortable. "You want to go for dinner or something? Have you eaten?"

I go crazy. I practically yell at the guy. "You think just because I tell you I'm a secretary I'm an easy lay?"

And then I remember what's going on and I laugh and laugh and can't stop.

Chapter 7

He's staring at me like he don't know whether to smile or run. Then he's leading me through the rooms, through the people, past the guard, down the staircase, outside. I'm still laughing. By now, he's laughing too, like he's in on the joke. I'm getting quiet, see him trying to hail a cab.

"No way," I tell him. "I ain't getting into no cab with you." By now I'm sobered up.

He looks hurt. "Okay," he says. "But let me have your number. I have a bad feeling you're not going to call me."

"Because I'm some kind of a nut?" And I start off again. This time he's not laughing.

"Everybody's crazy, Tina. You just have to find someone who's crazy in the same way you are. I think that's all there is to happiness."

And I'm thinking, we're a couple of loonies—me roaring like an idiot in the middle of the sidewalk, getting looks, and him talking at me like a fucking professor or something. Shit, I like the sound of his voice, though. But no way I'm going with him now. The guy could be a smooth talker, spots a little secy, figures he's got it made. Suspicious, that's me.

"Look, Noah, I will call you sometime, okay? Only a lot's going on right now."

"When?"

"When what?"

"When will you call?"

"Ain't that what girls always say?"

"I don't know. Is it?"

He's being cute. "Look, I'll call in a couple of days, okay?"

"Okay."

"So okay. So good night."

"Which way are you headed?"

"None of your business."

He smiles. "Good night, Tina. Please call me." He watches me walk off. I go up one block, then circle back. I'm not taking no chances.

All the way home I'm thinking about this guy. I'm already having fantasies this Noah's gonna be happy or something to find out I'm pregnant with some other guy's kid: Oh, Tina, I'm not able to have children. I will love him like he's my own.

That's what women do. I mean, I'm busy marrying the guy and all he's probably thinking is how soon can he get me into bed and how soon can he dump me after. Why God made men and women so different, I'll never know. I mean, it's a miracle anyone ever gets together.

Tina, I aks myself, what do you want? And that's a tough question. I mean, who knows what the hell they want? It's easier to know what you don't want. Me, I don't wanna work as a secretary. I don't wanna live in New Jersey. I guess I'd like a kid, but I don't want no husband. I guess that don't make no sense. I wanna see Noah again.

I know I should be sad or upset or something, but right now, I'm looking at the people on the train, people going home, happy to be going home, it's summer, the air-conditioning is working for a change. You be unhappy.

Chapter 8

The phone's ringing and I know it's Vinnie. Can't even get home and take a shower, he's checking up on me.

"Tina, where you been? You had me worried. I bet you went shopping."

"Maybe I did, maybe I didn't. Shit, Vinnie, get off my back."

"Hey, watch your mouth. We supposed to have dinner or what? It's fucking eight-thirty. I'm starving."

"Take it easy. We'll eat. Give me a half hour."

"Half hour shit. I'm coming over now."

"Okay, okay. Keep your shirt on."

"I was kind of hoping you'd tell me to take it off."

"Hey, I thought you was hungry."

"I am. Just thought I'd eat a little something if you know what I mean."

I hate when he does that. "Ha. Ha. Real funny. You really have a great sense of humor, you know that?"

"Don't get sarcastic with me, Tina. Sometimes you think you're real hot shit, you know that?"

"I am hot shit."

"Just get off the phone. I'm coming over."

One person I don't wanna see right now is Vinnie. 'Cause I gotta tell him and then he'll say let's get married like he's wanted to do all along. Sometimes I think I'm crazy. Maybe Angie's right. You get knocked up and here's the guy willing to marry you and you say no. That stuff's all right for movie stars, but not real people.

So now I'm getting ready for Vinnie and thinking maybe I should say yes. I mean, the guy loves me. He wouldn't hurt a fly. Not that he couldn't. I mean, he's big. I kid him sometimes he don't need tools to fix the pipes, if you know what I mean.

So I'm feeling good about him now. And when he shows I give him a big kiss and he wants to fool around but then I don't feel like it. I'm so hungry my stomach hurts.

"Look, Vinnie," I says, "I got something to tell you and then let's go out quick, I'm so hungry. Maybe we should order in."

Vinnie laughs. "What's with you, you pregnant or something?"

And it's not the way I planned it but I says yeah. Yeah, I am.

I can tell he's so happy he feels like doing a dance or something. "That's great! I'm gonna be a daddy!"

"Shh. The neighbors'll hear."

"So let them hear. I wanna tell everybody. We'll get married soon as possible. And I don't care, a boy or a girl. You know that, Tina. Whichever it is. Next time we'll try for the other."

Now I'm mad. "Next time? This one ain't even born yet. Just take it easy, okay, Vinnie? You're always doing that. You take things for granted, you know that?"

But he's too happy to fight. He just looks at me with this stupid grin on his face. "I'll make you happy, Teen, I swear it."

And he's got me crying. I mean, it's like a line from a movie, all he knows how to say, but the guy's sweet. You gotta give him that.

"Anything you want, Tina. I love you."

I just give him this sick smile. I don't know what to say, he's so happy. He thinks I want a big diamond and a raised ranch.

"Let's just go and get some food and bring it back, okay?"

But when we get back, it's worse, 'cause he's just kissing me all over the place until I kiss him back, all hot. And he touches me the way I like it, soft, on my breasts, and I'm wet, and I slide down to lick him, but he pulls away 'cause he's so excited, and climbs on top of me and I open my legs wide and we both come quick and it's good, better than it's been, but I feel bad 'cause it's not what I wanted, and now I know I'll never get rid of him.

Chapter 9

Going into work all I'm thinking is I gotta talk to Fern, which is weird, 'cause usually all the time I'm thinking I gotta talk to Angie, but this time I know Angie won't understand.

She keeps coming by my desk though, like she needs something—a layout, the length of a feature—but I know it's an excuse. She's trying to make up for yesterday.

"I ain't mad, Ange," I tell her. "And you better get some work done before you have Frieda the witch breathing down your neck."

"Oh, her. I ain't afraid of her. She don't dare say nothing to Marv or anyone about me. I been here too long."

"Hey, nobody's safe. Remember when they got rid of Carol last year? One day they wake up they don't like the color of your lipstick, you're history."

"Carol had a mouth. She said the wrong things to the wrong people."

"Oh, not like you and me, right? We ain't opened a mouth to just about everybody here?"

She laughs. "Yeah, but it's different. Everyone likes us. You and me—we're popular."

"Yeah, like it's high school. This place is like being back in fucking high school. You have to get here at a certain time, sit at your desk, do your work, not talk too much, you get a lousy hour for lunch, aks permission for everything. But if you're popular, you get away with certain shit."

Ange sighs. "Oh, Tina, why is everything always a story with you? You get paid, don't you?"

"What I make, it's like getting allowance."

She lets out a laugh and goes back to her department, which is Production. She knows everything that goes on, better than the salesmen, better than Marv, her boss. Somebody calls up to change an ad, Ange knows where to find it, when it came in, when it got set, what it cost, how many times it's running. All the time the salesmen are calling her: Ange, what about this agency, what's the story on this company? Fucking right Frieda better not say nothing about her.

Anyways, the only reason I got even two minutes to talk this morning is 'cause my boss, Lynn, is traveling again, at some stupid convention, and I say thank Christ for that. You never saw anyone so two-faced. I mean, the guy comes on all sweetness and you think maybe he's nice and kind 'cause of his limp and someone who really cares, ya know? He'll promise you anything. I always think about that old commercial: *Promise her anything.* But you look in your little envelope for the raise, it's always, "Next month." I mean, he gives me the creeps. Got no use for women except as fucking servants. One time his wife comes in. She brings up this roll and butter from the lunch room. He makes her get down on her hands and knees and clean up the crumbs.

Fern is the first girl he hired as a reporter. Only time I ever seen Dave, the publisher, fight him for something. Anyways, Lynn was in his office giving Dave the bull about how a girl wouldn't understand shit about computers and stuff and I'm laughing 'cause I'm looking at her résumé and she's fucking Phi Beta Kappa. Oh, I know the dirt all right. Maybe that's why they go easy on me.

I'm typing this same letter all morning. I'm bursting to

talk and I'm so hungry I can't think straight. Finally Fern comes by and says is now good and I stand right up and says an hour ago was good.

She must be doing an interview this afternoon 'cause she's wearing this dark suit and little heels and usually she shows up in pants. So I tell her she looks nice and she thanks me but don't return the compliment and I'm wondering if I look like shit. And I worry I got my clothes wrong again and then remember I'm gonna be big as a house soon and what the hell will it matter.

She picks an Indian restaurant and I don't say no. There's funny music playing and dirty pictures hanging all over. I guess in India, that's art or something. I feel a little weird, but I'm so hungry I don't care where I am. Only thing is, I don't know what the hell to order. "Help me out here, Fern," I says, and she suggests stuff and I'm saying fine 'cause I just want food in my mouth.

"So what's going on?" she says. "Or is this about the promotion?"

"What promotion?"

"Well, not promotion, but job change. But he's sure to give you more money."

"What the hell are you talking about?"

"Come on, Tina. You must have heard something. Chris is leaving and Dave wants you to be his secretary."

"Holy shit."

"Well, it shouldn't be a surprise. Everyone knows you're really smart and all. Have you thought any more about going to college, Tina? There's no telling what you could do."

I give her a face like tell me another one.

"Well, maybe it's none of my business. But, really, you didn't know about the job with Dave?"

"No. I guess I been thinking of other things lately."

"Well," she says, and colors a little. "Don't tell anyone I told you, but I think there's a good chance. Then you don't have to work for Lynn anymore."

I'm eating something like a fried banana and drinking

beer and worried maybe I shouldn't be drinking beer 'cause that's like a drink, ain't it? And I feel like I don't know what's going on. This time I really blew it. Go and get myself fucking knocked up just when I'm about to get a decent job.

Fern's looking at me hard. "If you didn't know about the job, then this must be about the doctor."

I nod and surprise myself by reaching for her hand. "Fern, I'm gonna tell you something you gotta swear if your mother on her deathbed begged you to tell her, you wouldn't say a word."

She stares at me like I'm crazy, and I feel like maybe I am.

"Okay, Fern?"

She kind of pats my hand and nods. "Okay, Tina, what's going on?"

So I tell her. And she don't say this, that, or the other thing. Just aks me how I feel about it.

"I don't know," I says. But I smile. I mean, when someone says the right thing, it's like they gave you this gift.

"What do you think I should do?" I aks her.

"Well, you have a lot of options. You could keep the baby, put it up for adoption, or have an abortion. No one can tell you what's best for you."

"I don't know if I could kill this baby."

"Don't look at it that way."

"How else can you look at it?"

Her voice gets funny so I'm not sure I hear her exactly. "It's too little to be anything, yet. It's a bunch of cells without thought or feeling. If you're in no position to raise a child properly, isn't it better, kinder, to eliminate it at this point?"

"Jesus, Fern, I guess I touched a nerve."

She sniffs. "Please don't tell a soul, Teen. No one, okay? But I had an abortion a couple of years ago."

I can't believe it. "My God, Fern. Did the guy know?"

"What does that matter?"

"I don't know. I guess I just wondered."

"Well, he knew all right."

"It must of been rough."

"I did what I had to do."

I don't say nothing.

"Do you think I did the wrong thing?"

"Christ, Fern. I don't know. Was it the wrong thing?"

"Maybe." She's kind of sobbing. "I mean, I sure wasn't going to marry anyone, I didn't have the money to raise a kid by myself, and I wanted to work. But I go around with this aching where the baby should have been."

"So why do you say it's a choice for me?"

"Because it still might be the best choice. Maybe it was for me. I guess I'm just saying it's not an easy choice."

"Maybe I should have the baby and give it up."

"If you think you can do that."

I smile. "I don't know. Maybe not. I mean, when I was a kid, I wasn't too good at sharing toys. I wouldn't let my sister play with my dolls. I guess I don't much like the idea of having strangers raise my baby. I mean, how can you be sure they're all right? You make mistakes with a kid, at least they're your mistakes. How would I know if they loved my baby?"

Fern is drying her eyes. "Tina, you sound like you want this baby."

I'm groggy from the beer. The food is little bits of meat in greasy sauce but it tastes good. It tastes delicious.

"I don't know. But I don't wanna kill the baby. I don't wanna give away the baby. But Vinnie, my boyfriend, he wants to get married, and I don't. I mean, maybe it's crazy, but, I have the baby myself, I still have my life. I marry Vinnie—I love him in a way, he's a really nice guy—but I don't have my life no more. I have his life. His kid."

"But how will you keep the baby? I mean, do you have someone to watch him while you work? Your mother or something?"

I laugh. My mother. Right. "No, she's back living with my grandmother. It's a long story."

"You'll find a way, Tina. But meanwhile, don't say anything. Take the job with Dave if he offers it to you. Get away from Lynn. He's just a pig. Sometimes I ask myself why I stay."

It's when we go to pay that I find the card in my purse and remember about Noah. I stand looking at it until Fern aks me what the matter is.

"Things are so crazy," I whisper. "I mean, here I am pregnant, with a guy wants to marry me, and I meet this guy last night." I show her the card.

"He gave you his business card? God, I hate when they do that."

"Well, I didn't want him to call me or anything. So he said I should call him."

Fern laughs. "Tina, you're something. Look, you don't want this guy, give him my number. Unless he's married. I've had enough of married guys if you know what I mean."

"I didn't say I didn't want him."

She can't believe her ears. "You're going to see him? I mean, is this the time to start a new relationship?"

"Who knows? I'm making it up as I go along."

"I guess we all do, Tina. Let me know what happens."

We walk back to work. And, I don't know, maybe I'm a little drunk from the beer, but inside it's all gray. No colors in the whole building. The people, coming back inside from lunch, go from bright to dull as they push through the revolving door.

Chapter 10

It's after five on a Wednesday on a slow news week and almost everyone has gone home. I can't wait no more. I go into Lynn's empty office and close the door. I'm so excited about calling this guy I feel hot. I haven't felt this way for a long time.

"Johnson, Latzman, and Shapiro," the receptionist sing-songs. "I'm sorry, Mr. Lieb has left for the day. Is there any message?"

Now I feel like a jerk. What the hell am I doing anyway? I say no, hang up, and quickly dial Jeanette's number.

"Hi, kid. What's up? You gonna come all the way out here in the middle of the week? What, Vinnie away or something?"

"No. It has nothing to do with Vinnie. I just wanna see you. You and the kids."

"Suit yourself. Nicky works late tonight so it's okay."

"It's not okay for your sister to come if he's not working late?"

"Don't start in again, Tina. Nick likes you okay. But you always get into an argument. I don't need yelling, you know? You wanna come over, come over. But you better sleep here. I don't want you taking no bus by yourself at night."

I don't wanna bother stopping home on the way. I just wanna be there. So I go to Bolton's to buy a new dress to wear tomorrow. It's navy. Just plain with a white collar. Classy. I buy it big.

Jeanette's got one of them yellow kitchens. I mean, it's pretty, I guess, but everything's yellow—the wallpaper, the floor, the dish towels—everything matches. Like once she got started she couldn't stop herself. All yellow. But she's proud of her potholders and appliance covers with these little kitchen-type pictures on them. You know. Coffeepots with flowers stuck in 'em and shit like that. We'll get on the phone and she'll tell me, "I saw the cutest little salt and peppers, just what I been looking for, but they were out of 'em so the girl said she could order it from their other store or maybe did I wanna go over there?" I mean, she spends a lot of time on this stuff.

How else is she gonna fill the day? The kids are a lot of work, but Donna's in school now and Nick's mother thinks up any excuse to come over and watch the baby. Jeannie loves her kids, but I think sometimes women have children just so's they'll have something to do.

I know Jeannie would like a little job. But you wanna hear something? Nick won't let her work. I mean, I would laugh if it wasn't so fucking sad. I think she's building up to it, though. She wants to work in one of them mall stores. Gift items. She'd be good at it, too.

So I'm sitting in her yellow kitchen while Joey crawls around our feet and Donna's in the family room watching *Mr. Mom* or some shit for the tenth time on the VCR and Jeannie's looking at me like I'm nuts because of the dress in the bag. "You couldn't of gone home? I would of kept supper for you, Tina." She shakes her head. "Sometimes you act crazy, you know that?"

"I must be crazy, Jeannie," I says. "I'm pregnant."

Then she's up on her feet and hollering she's so happy.

"You're what? By Vinnie? How far along?" She picks up the baby and hugs him. "Oh, Teen! Now you'll have a normal life!"

"Whaddaya mean normal?"

"Come on, Tina, you know what I mean. Get married. Have babies. A family."

"Like you."

"Yeah, like me. I didn't do so bad."

"I didn't say nothing."

"Yeah, I know what you think, Miss Big-Deal Working Girl."

"Shit, Jean, I didn't come here to fight with you."

She comes over to kiss me. She smells so good. So warm with some toilet water or splash or something I can just pick up the scent of.

"Jeannie, listen, I'm thinking of maybe not marrying Vinnie. I don't wanna. I'll have the baby and figure something out."

She sits back down, staring at me.

"That is the stupidest thing I ever heard. You know something? You're a little dope. Yeah, you heard me. You think you know everything and you don't know nothing. Already thirty years old and listen to her. You don't care what people say? You don't care what people think? Have you told Pop? I'm sure he'll really go for this idea. You wanna kill him?"

"Don't give me that shit, Jean. This has nothing to do with Pop. It's my life. He won't want me to marry Vinnie if I don't love him."

She's shaking her head. "Yeah, what he really wants is a little bastard grandchild. Is that what all his hard work'll come to?"

"If you're gonna be so fucking helpful I'll just leave, okay? Forget I said anything. I don't need your advice!"

"Where you going, big shot? Who the hell else is gonna help you? Your fancy friends at the office? Maybe if you would of kept up with your old friends . . ."

"Those creeps? Jesus, Jean, what the hell are you bringing that up for? Besides, I don't need no help." But I'm crying.

She comes over again. "Look, kid, don't make any big decisions right off, okay? A guy like Vinnie don't come around every day. A guy who loves you, is good to you. A nice-looking guy, makes a good living. Look, a baby needs a father. It's his kid. You can't take his kid away from him."

"I'm not going nowhere. He can see the kid. But if I marry him I'll never do anything else as long as I live."

I'm sorry as soon as I say that 'cause she takes it personally. She sits down exhausted.

"I didn't mean nothing, Jeannie."

She's not angry, just sad. "What do you think life is anyway, Teen?" But then she shuts up 'cause Donna comes into the room.

"Mommy, I'm hungry."

"If you would of eaten your supper maybe you wouldn't be hungry."

"But Aunt Tina said I didn't have to if I didn't want to."

"And I said eat it or starve."

"Please, Mommy?" She's a cute kid with dirty-blond curls and she's in this Barbie nightgown with big floppy slippers. Jean fixes her a glass of milk and some kind of sandwich.

"What's that?" I aks Jean.

"Ketchup."

"Ketchup and what?"

"Ketchup and bread." She turns to Donna. "Finish up and brush your teeth."

"Ah, Ma, I wanna stay up with you and Aunt Tina."

"Listen, young lady, it's a school night. It's already past your bedtime. So get moving."

"Can Aunt Tina tell me a story?"

"Sure, kid," I says. "But listen to your mom."

"Your wish is my command."

We laugh as she leaves. Where does she pick it up?

Jean's shaking her head. "First grade. And already it's girlfriends and boyfriends. This one likes that one. This one kissing the other one."

"Yeah? Donna have a boyfriend?"

"Who knows? She don't talk to me."

"She's a great kid, Jean."

Jeannie smiles. She loves it when I say nice stuff about Donna, but she's always yelling at her.

She's gonna follow her upstairs but then Nick comes home and gives me that "What are you doing here?" look. Maybe he's not the worst guy in the world, but he's bad enough.

"You been here all day or what, Tina?"

"Hello to you, too, Nick."

"What's it matter how long she been here?"

"He's worried maybe I ate two meals here."

"Come on, Tina, Nick didn't mean nothing, did you, Nick?"

"Never mind what I meant."

Jeannie takes the baby and leaves the room to go up to Donna. I used to think she tried to leave Nick and me together a lot to give us time to be friends, but now I think it's 'cause she don't know what the hell to do in the same room with the both of us.

"You still working the same job, Nick?"

"Yeah."

"How's it going?"

"Okay."

I don't know why I bother.

He's sitting at the table in his plaster-streaked clothes eating the sausage and peppers Jean kept warm for him. "This tastes like shit," he says. Like he knows the difference between that and food.

"I thought it was pretty good."

"What do you know? You don't cook."

"Sure I cook."

"Yeah, right. You can't boil water. You ever find a husband, I pity the guy."

Then he laughs. Why do these dumb guys always think they're so funny? You insult someone, it's being clever.

I go upstairs. Jeannie's still fighting Donna. "Right now, young lady, this minute. No, you can't wear your new dress to bed. Donna, one more word and I'll have your father up here."

"Aunt Tina, Aunt Tina, tell me a story!"

Jeannie rolls her eyes. "Just don't make it too long, Teen. She's gotta get up for school tomorrow." She kisses Donna. "Good night, honey bunny."

I love Donna's room. It's like a little girl's room in a magazine. All pink-and-white checks and stuffed animals lined up everywhere and ruffly curtains. It's like a joke when you think of what me and Jeannie had growing up. I mean, Pop did his best, but we had fucking plastic paneling in our bedroom.

"Tell me the story about Grandma Joan."

"Naw. How about something about a princess or something?"

"Uh-uh."

"All right, honey." She always aks for this. I don't think Jean talks to her about Ma.

"Well, when Grandma Joan was a teenager, almost a grown-up, she was very beautiful, and many, many men wanted to marry her. But one day Grandpa Sal came into the grocery store where she worked and she was helping somebody else and she dropped some eggs. And Grandpa Sal helped her clean them up and told her a beautiful girl like that shouldn't have to get her hands dirty. And she always said how she knew he would be good to her and that's why she decided to marry him, even though her parents and his parents didn't want them to."

"Because of the differences."

"Because of the differences. But they cried and carried on and finally their parents—your great-grandparents— said okay and everybody said what a beautiful bride Grandma Joan was. Now go to sleep."

"But that's not the whole story."

"Mommy said to keep it short."

"Please, Aunt Tina."

"Another time, sweetie."

"Please, Aunt Tina, I won't be able to go to sleep without the whole story and then I'll stay up and be scared."

Who can say no to a kid? "Okay, sweetie. So they got married and pretty soon a beautiful baby girl was born."

"That was Mommy!"

"That was your mommy. And a little while after that a skinny, ugly baby girl was born."

"That was you, Aunt Tina!"

"That was me. And soon after that Grandma Joan started to not feel well. Everybody said it was like she was under some kind of spell."

"Like from a bad witch, right?"

"Right. Like that. She talked funny and couldn't remember stuff."

"Like what? What funny stuff did she say?"

"I don't know, honey. I was too little to remember."

"Silly things like *kapowkablouiehaha?*"

"What's that?"

"Just stuff Billy says in school."

"Billy your boyfriend?"

"Never mind. Anyway, Mom says I'm too young to have a boyfriend."

"And she's right. Well, anyways, then Grandma Joan had to go to a special place to make her better and Grandpa Sal had to take care of his two little girls by himself. And sometimes Grandma Joan came home, but mostly she didn't, and she still isn't all well and that's why she lives with Great-Grandma and that's why we don't see her too much."

"Mommy had another baby. Is Mommy gonna get sick?"

"Oh, no, honey. Just 'cause Grandma Joan got sick don't mean Mommy will get sick."

"How do you know?"

"I just know. Now that's the story. Go to sleep. I love you."

"I love you too, Aunt Tina. Could you live with us?"

"Oh, honey, I don't think so, but thanks for aksing. Sweet dreams."

"Sweet dreams, Aunt Tina."

When I go back down, Nick's already getting ready for bed. He works a lot. He's what people would call a good husband: If a guy don't drink, don't hit you, don't fool around, and makes a living, he's a real catch. Like if you got that, you got everything.

Jean gives me a look like we better not talk no more. No fooling. I whisper that she better swear not to tell Nick. "How'm I gonna keep it a secret, Teen?" But she promises to keep her mouth shut for a while.

Jeannie's made up the den for me. I like sleeping on the sofa bed. Jeannie has special sheets just for it, and they always smell fresh. I lie there thinking about Noah, making up scenes about how crazy he is about me and stuff and getting myself hot. So I get up and go into the kitchen and open the fridge. I'm standing in one of Jeanette's night-gowns, with the light from inside flooding over me, staring at the Tupperware. This baby's hungry.

In the morning, I hear Nick in the kitchen at 6:00 A.M. I can tell he's trying to be quiet, and suddenly I feel like I could love him. Not like him. That's aksing too much. But he's my sister's husband and Donna and Joey's father and I'm stuck with him. I get up after he leaves, shower, put my new dress on. I feel like this is the first day of the rest of my life as a pregnant lady.

I hear Donna and Jeannie fighting upstairs. Donna don't wanna go to school. Jean comes down in tears, the baby wriggling in her arms. "The same thing every morning. I give up. She loves school. She does real well. But she never wants to go. She can't stand that Joey's home with me and she's not. But what the hell can I do?"

Donna comes in in this little sundress I bought her, a purple headband bunching up her curls. She looks thirteen or something. "Honey," I says, "you don't go to school, no one's gonna see how good you look."

"You going to work, Aunt Tina?"

"I better be, kiddo."

"Aw, Teen," Jeannie says, "I was hoping you'd stay with me."

I wanna stay, I don't wanna go nowhere. But I shake my head and take the baby from her. I hold his soft, warm body against me.

"He's drooling on your new dress, Teen."

"That's okay," I tell her.

Chapter 11

Riding back to the city, I'm making a list in my head. People I gotta tell. I guess Pop's next. Ma can wait. Who knows if she'll even understand what I'm saying, and if she does, what the hell can she say to me? She made a mess of her life. She can't yell at me for nothing.

Of course today because I gave myself so much time to get here I'm early, and there's that friggin' Frieda standing in the lobby waiting for the elevator. Shit. I hate that. I should read just so's I can make like I didn't see her with my face stuck in a book or newspaper. I figure they don't start paying me till I turn down that last hallway leading to the office. Up till then, my time's my own.

That's what's so shitty about working. You gotta spend time with all these people you can't stand and pretend to like 'em on top of that. That's why Carol got kicked out. She told people off. You gotta keep it to yourself till you bust.

Frieda don't look too thrilled to see me neither. Gives me one of them little jabs with her chin she thinks is hello. What the hell is up her ass, anyways? I mean, okay, so she's real short and kind of stocky, not everybody's type, but her face ain't half-bad. Close to fifty, I bet, never married. There's plenty worse find husbands if they want to. If she wasn't so goddamn grouchy all the time maybe she would of.

"My, you're early today, Tina. And a new dress, too."

I try to smile but I can tell I didn't make it. I mean, even in kindergarten my teacher didn't talk to me like that.

"I bet something's up," she says, making herself smile for all she's worth to try to pull it out of me. Like I'm gonna tell her shit. Now I give her a big grin, 'cause she obviously don't know about the job and she'll be good and mad when she finds out later, and I'm pretty happy about that. I just look around the elevator like I can't discuss my private business in front of all these people and she gives me another one of those jabs like, oh, *she* understands, and I'm ready to crack up.

We get off and she's gonna jump on me again but we run into all these guys bringing the carpeting and she gets all busy telling them what they're doing wrong. Then I know who chose the color. I mean, Dave's the boss, I guess, but sometimes you'd think she is. It's funny the way sometimes people are afraid of people they don't have to be afraid of. How many times have people gotten into fights because of her and I know Dave hates that. I mean, he could fucking fire her, but he don't. He lets her pick the carpeting.

Dave's standing around my desk, sort of half reading some stuff on top and acting real nervous. I know what's going on. Lynn's out of the office for a week and that's why Dave found the guts to talk to me.

"Oh, hi, Tina!" he says all startled like I'm the last person in the world he expected to see. Then he says real quick and low that since Chris is leaving and all and seeing as how he'll need a new secretary and that I seem like such a responsible young woman unless of course I don't want to, if I'm happy where I am that's fine and he'll get somebody else. He's too much.

And I wanna tell him the truth. I wanna tell him he's

heading for a big fight with Lynn over me and I'm pregnant and one way or the other I'm gonna have to leave in about eight months. But I don't. I mean, I got at least another two months before I'm even showing.

By now most of the office is in and everyone's looking over at us. No one's got no privacy. Lynn sits in front, checking up on everyone. Fern says it's like one of them slave ships in the old movies. You know. The slave driver sits up front beating out a rhythm on a drum and the slaves row for all they're worth.

I don't know, maybe Lynn's such a prick 'cause he's got this limp from someplace, no one knows from where, whether he was born that way or what. He don't talk about it, so I don't think he was no war hero or nothing like that. I felt sorry for him at first, but it ain't no excuse. You'd think it'd make him understand other people got troubles too. But no way.

Fern is sending out this big smile, but Angie looks worried. I signal to meet her in the Ladies.

"What's going on, Teen?"

"You don't know?"

"If I knew, would I need you to tell me?"

"Dave wants me to be his secretary."

"Wow. Great. But what about Lynn?"

"Screw'm."

She laughs. "Well, you gonna take it?"

"Of course."

"But what about . . . ?"

"Nothing. Nothing about it. But what I wanna know is how come you never said nothing to me? You always know everything."

"Don't look at me. Why didn't Tony tell you?"

"Oh, come on, Ange. He's just the bullshit managing editor. Nobody ever tells him nothing."

"So why you jumping down my throat? Nobody knew."

"Fern knew."

"Fern knew?" Angie raises her eyebrows. "That's interesting."

"Whaddaya mean?"

"You figure it out."

"Come *on*, Angie. Fern and Dave?"

"Why not?"

"He's married for Chrissake!"

She looks at me like she never saw nobody so stupid in her whole life. "So?"

And then it makes sense, and I'm about to tell her what Fern said about married men, but then Rochelle comes in looking for Ange, and I'm glad I didn't.

"Congratulations, Tina," Rochelle says, and looks like she's gonna kiss me, but I pull away. I just can't warm up to her. She's like a little dog or something, always trying to get you to pet her.

When they leave, I take out my brush and stand in front of the mirror just brushing and brushing my hair till it hurts. I don't feel like going out yet. I like it in here. The pink tile with gray trim, the little soap dispensers by each sink, the flickering fluorescent bulb. The shelf where the girls are always forgetting letters they were on their way to copy, or rings, or combs, or makeup. It's like a fucking home away from home.

Chapter 12

Two minutes after I get back to my desk Vinnie calls, so mad he could spit: Where was I last night? What's going on? He's gonna kill me. I tell him about the new job.

"What?" he screams into the phone. "What the fuck are you talking about? I'm not interested in your fucking job. Where were you? I called your father I was so worried."

"You did what?"

"I called Sal."

"What the hell is wrong with you?"

"*Me?* What the hell is wrong with *you?*"

"Vinnie, I can't talk to you now. I'm at work."

I hang up. I know I'm wrong. Here's a guy loves me, already loves the baby—I treat him like shit. But he won't leave me alone.

After work, I go find Pop. I like walking in the old neighborhood. It smells good, like pizza and the ocean all mixed up together. I know every store: the shoemaker; the two bakeries, one for bread and the other for cake; the fruit stand. Each one I pass I think: What would they say if they knew? What would Mrs. Maldonado say? What would Uncle Louie say? They'll be talking about me in the fish store soon enough.

The blood smell of the meat hits me when I go into the market and I feel like I'm gonna keel over. Ralph and Mario, almost hidden behind the hanging sausage and piles of cheese, call to me from behind the counter. "Tina! *Bellissima! Come va?*"

Like shit, I think, but I tell them, *"Va bene."* It's about all the Italian I know. They'll go jabbering at me for an hour and then be shocked I don't know what the hell they're talking about.

"You looking for your pop?" Ralph points to the back.

Pop's sitting in the stockroom having a smoke. How many times did I beg him to stop? But Pop, he needs something in his hand to hang on to.

He's wearing his white coat stained with blood and one of them baseball-type hats in brown and yellow. His says "House O' Weenies." He's dropping his ashes into the sawdust. All the time, growing up, there was sawdust on the floor he tracked in. Aunt Vicky would come over and clean, she'd complain about it. "For God's sake, Sal, wipe your feet!"

He gives me a big smile. "Hey, stranger." He always says that. Funny thing, today it's like true. I ain't seen him in a week, but it feels like forever.

He's getting fat. I'm worried about him. But now he's got a new wife to do the worrying, so I don't say nothing.

"You know Vinnie called me yesterday. What the hell was that about?"

"He thinks he's my keeper."

"Hey, he's a nice boy."

I've had it. "Not you too, Pop."

"Listen, Tina. You don't want him, that's one thing. Just tell him. Don't take nobody you don't want. But don't go keep him hanging around, neither."

"I'm not trying to break up with him, Pop. I'm gonna marry him."

He gives me a big smile. He's happy. I'm making him happy.

"Whaddaya know!" He kisses me. "Let me tell those big shots in there," he says, putting out his smoke. I know he's been waiting for this for years. Finally I'm respectable. He can boast about me.

"Better wait a minute, Pop."

"You got something else to tell me?"

"I'm gonna have a baby, Pop."

He blushes, but he's still smiling. "So don't say it like it's something bad! I can always use another grandchild!"

I hug him 'cause I don't wanna look at him. "I'm scared, Pop," I tell his shoulder.

"Naw. You'll be okay. My girls turned out okay."

"Sure, Pop."

"You know, when you and your sister was growing up, I always worried that one of you would, well, you know, would go a little wild like your mother. Every time something happened, a fight, an argument, I thought maybe this is it. Maybe this is how it starts."

"But I'm scared of getting married, scared of having a baby."

"Oh," he says. "That's nothing. That's just normal."

I aks myself what's the use. But I try one more time.

"I'm not sure I love Vinnie, Pop."

He pulls away and lights another cigarette. "We don't get no guarantees, Tina." I don't say nothing and he looks up at me like he's gonna cry or something. "Vinnie's a nice guy."

And I smile down at him. "Sure, Pop," I says. "Sure."

Chapter 13

When I get home, Vinnie's truck is parked outside the building: DOPODOMANI PLUMBING. And all of a sudden it hits me that's gonna be my name. Unless I don't change it, which I'm sure Vinnie'll go for in a big way.

I'm sorry I ever gave him a key. There he is, sitting in the living room reading *People*. I can't have no privacy. But at least he's not mad no more. He's looking at me like he don't wanna say nothing to start me off. When I smile, he practically crumbles in relief.

"I just went to see Pop," I tell him.

"Yeah?"

"Yeah."

I'm driving him crazy.

"So you tell him anything?"

"About us?"

"Yeah about us. Jesus, Teen."

"Maybe I said something. Maybe I said we was getting married."

Then he's hugging me and twirling me around. Then like in a movie he stops and looks at me all serious. "I guess I shouldn't of done that."

"Why the hell not?"

"Because of the baby."

"Oh, shit, Vinnie. Don't you know nothing? That's a lot of hooey. You can't hurt the baby, which is about the size of a raisin right now, by stuff like that."

"Whaddaya mean, a raisin?"

"A raisin. I don't mean it *is* a raisin, stupid. I mean it starts out like nothing and then gets bigger."

"Oh."

I can tell he never thought about it before. How can you get to be thirty-two years old and not know shit about babies? I mean, Vinnie wasn't exactly sitting on his hands before he started going with me, if you know what I mean. I guess it's just guys, or guys like Vinnie. Usually that kind of thing gets me crazy, but tonight I'm gonna let it pass. If I let every little thing he does bother me, I'll never go through with this.

"How come you know all this stuff?" he aks me.

"Women know stuff like that."

"Yeah?"

"Yeah."

He comes over and pats my belly. I guess it's being pregnant, or maybe not having to think about using nothing, but I get hot the second he puts a hand on me.

"You can't get another one in there, can you?"

"Good Christ, Vin, you really don't know shit." I sort of push him off, but he can tell I don't mean it. We don't even bother taking all our clothes off, just do it right there on the chair. I'm so wet I don't even need him to touch me. But I'm not thinking of him.

After, he's kissing my sweaty hair. "See? I told you getting married was a good idea."

I nod. I'm in no position to disagree.

"When Tina?"

"I guess it better be soon."

He lifts me off and all of a sudden he's all business. "We got a million things to think of, Teen."

"Like what?" I call back on the way to the bathroom.

"Whaddaya mean, like what? Like the wedding and buying a house. That's like what."

"Don't go buying no house."

"Why not?"

"We gotta talk about it first. You don't know nothing about buying no houses."

"And I suppose you do?"

"I know more than you."

"Right."

I come out mad. "Look, Vinnie, before you met me, you never even been outta Brooklyn."

"So what does that have to do with anything? Besides, they got anything so special in Manhattan? And for your information, I go there plenty."

"Yeah. And all you see is the underneath of somebody's sink."

"Yeah? Well let me tell you, I happen to meet a lot of different people. A nice class of people, too. So don't go giving me your shit, Tina."

"Well what good did it ever do you? What did you ever learn from it?"

"I learned this. That I got my own goddamn business with two guys working for me and I do a good fucking job. What makes you so great? You know something? Not everybody got the same ideas as you. You know that?"

I don't say nothing, but I give him a look.

He can't stay mad. "Look, Tina, we'll talk about it. I won't do nothing about a house without telling you. I just thought you'd like something near Jeanette."

I have to smile. I thought he was gonna say near *his* sister. Still. "Well, just hold off, okay? I don't know what I want yet."

"Well you better think about it."

Now I'm angry again. "Don't tell me what I should do, Vinnie. I'm telling you not to buy a fucking house. Besides, where do you come off talking about buying a house?"

"I got the money. Don't worry about it."

Funny, I never thought about how much money Vinnie's got, and I guess he never talked to me about it. "Please, Vinnie. Just don't do it, okay?"

"Okay, sure," he says, smiling. "We'll have a discussion."

But I can see his mind's made up. "Look," I says, "just let me do the wedding."

"No problem, Tina. That's the bride's thing. But just remember I got a big family. And a lot of people to invite because of the business. We don't wanna hurt nobody's feelings."

"Vin*nie*! There ain't time to plan no big wedding."

"Tina, use your head. You make a small wedding, you might as well make a big one."

"I thought you said the wedding was the bride's thing."

"Yeah, yeah. Whatever you want."

Right. Whatever I fucking want.

He goes over to the mirror to comb his hair.

"Just one thing, Vinnie," I says, looking at him. "You gotta buy a new fucking suit."

Chapter 14

*L*ynn's back. Shit. I thought he'd be out all week. I should of known better. It gets close to deadline, he gets nervous. Like the place would fall apart if he wasn't there dragging himself around and breathing down everybody's neck.

And today he's really in a mood, what with the workmen trying to do their jobs, and of course he's making cracks about how dumb they are. So now it's hard to talk to Angie and tell her what's up. All morning she and Fern are passing by my desk giving me these looks like they're dying to know what's happening. It drives me crazy. When Ange comes around again I grab her and say we'll go to lunch at twelve.

Of course, Lynn hears this. "Just don't come back late. I know how it is when you girls start talking. You just lose track of the time."

In my mind, I punch him out. This fucker takes three-hour lunches whenever some PR guy from IBM or National Semiconductor or something blows into town, and he's afraid I might take five extra minutes on my measly hour.

Before I leave I go over to Dave. He blushes when he sees me, and before I get a word out he apologizes for not

53

talking to Lynn yet. "This afternoon, I promise." But with the way Dave runs things, I'm wondering maybe he'll never tell him.

Angie is busting. She practically pulls me all the way to Dim Sum & Den Sum. Before we go in she peeks in the window to make sure no one we know is there.

The waitress comes over. "Number nine and number four, right?"

"Right," Ange agrees, but I stop her.

"Maybe today I want something different. Could I see a menu?"

Ange shakes her head in disbelief. "Since when did you ever order anything but the shrimp in lobster sauce?"

"Since today." I choose another number without really looking. "You know, Ange, it ain't good to get stuck in a rut."

She lets it pass. "So?" She's got her eyes open so wide her forehead must hurt.

"So you better buy yourself a new dress."

She reaches up quick and squeezes my hand across the table. The little teacups rattle in their saucers. "I'm so happy, Teen. It's the right thing. It'll turn out wonderful, you'll see."

"I guess so, Ange."

"So whaddaya want?"

I don't get it. "Whaddaya mean?"

"The baby. A boy or a girl?"

"It don't matter."

"Come on, Tina. Can you be happy about this?"

"I am happy."

"Oh yeah?" she says, biting into some noodles. "If this is happy, I'd hate to see you at a funeral."

When we get back, I know something's up, 'cause Lynn is like ignoring me. Usually on a Friday he's finding a million things for me to do like call the plant eighty-nine times to make sure the copy came in right. So good for Dave. Something must of given him a kick in the pants.

Maybe Fern, 'cause she keeps smiling and nodding at me while she's on the phone doing some last-minute story.

Sure enough, by six we're closed, Lynn's getting his coat on and real sweet says to me, "So you've decided to take another job?"

He's waiting there all crooked for me to answer. He reminds me of when I was a kid and I was playing with a doll or some toy and wanted to make it stand up and couldn't, and so I had to open up the legs in some real crazy position to get it to balance.

"Ah, yeah," I finally tell him. "It kind of came up."

"Haven't you been happy where you were?"

He's too much. It's all I gotta do not to scream at him.

"Oh," I says, "real happy. Just thought I'd try something different for a while."

"I see."

It's like he's gonna explode he's so angry. But talking real nice the whole time. That's Lynn. A fucking two-face.

"Well, I guess I'll just have to get another girl. Maybe this one will make the coffee!"

He laughs like that's some kind of good joke.

"Well, Tina. I guess you won't mind sticking it out for a few more weeks till we get a new girl in here?"

"No, Lynn, that'll be fine."

"Good," he says between his teeth. "You go and have a nice weekend."

I watch him limp off, trying to walk real fast like nothing's bothering him, and I feel like shaking the guy. I mean, he's crazy. Treats me like a lump of shit, then I take another job, it's like I stabbed him in the back or I broke his heart or something. What a jerk. I mean, I think they should give some sort of sanity test before they let people become bosses.

Fern comes over to congratulate me. She's talking to me, but I see her watching Dave out of the corner of her eye. She's waiting to see when he'll leave. Jesus, I feel like a little dummy I never noticed nothing before.

I'm on my way out, but I don't wanna go home. I'm too

worked up. So I find myself rooting through my bag for Noah's card. I go to one of the phones in the lobby and call.

This time a man answers and I aks for him.

"That's me. How can I help you?"

"Oh, I kind of expected the receptionist."

"Sorry. Who's this, please?"

"It's Tina."

I hear him take a breath. "Great."

"How are you?"

"Fine. How are you?"

"Fine. I got a new job."

"Mazel tov."

"Well, just thought I'd call."

"Wait. Can we get together?"

"Sure. You wanna get a drink or something?"

"Sure."

So we make plans to meet at the Horse's Head, which is kind of midway, in a half hour. I'm so excited I'm flying. I know I'm acting nutty, but I wanna see him so bad.

I wait for the bus. I don't wanna be early, and I figure the bus'll be slower than walking. I mean, you wanna get somewhere in New York, you don't get on no bus. You wanna go sightseeing, that's a different story.

The bar is downstairs a couple of steps in one of them old-timey buildings been there forever, and it looks like they ain't fixed it up since day one. It's real smoky, and I guess what with that and all the Village types hanging out, it's kind of a cool place.

When I walk in, I feel like a dope. All these people standing around with drinks in their hands, talking a little loud, laughing like they never had a better time in their lives, looking everybody over. It's like a fucking party in junior high school.

But I see Noah sitting at the bar watching the door. I feel weak. I love the way this guy looks. He's tall, and not real comfortable perched on that little stool. His hair kind of a light brown, real fine, with a little bit falling across his forehead. A kind of long, pointy nose and eyes that crinkle up like now when he smiles. I'm so busy staring I don't move for a minute. He starts to get up and that wakes me.

"Hi, Tina. You look great."

"You, too. You look great, too."

He orders me a drink and I sit there playing with it taking maybe one sip 'cause I know I shouldn't drink it. But I keep wolfing down these pretzels.

We move over to a table and he aks me about the new job. But I don't wanna talk. I wanna look at him. So he starts talking, telling me what he does. But then I'm uncomfortable 'cause I don't really get it. I don't know what the fuck a shareholders' suit is and I'm too embarrassed to aks. I stare at his hands. Small hands for a pretty tall guy. I want to touch them.

He aks me again about the job and finally I start telling him about the office. About Lynn and Dave and Fern and Angie and Frieda. I even tell him about fucking Rochelle. I talk and talk all the time looking at him looking at me. And I think: This is ridiculous. I gotta level with this guy. I can't like start dating and one day tell him I can't see you next weekend 'cause I'm going on my honeymoon.

"Noah, what the hell is it you like about me?"

"I don't know, Tina. I guess I think you're beautiful. That night at the museum, looking at the paintings. You looked so lovely. And I felt, I don't know, some connection to you. Maybe that sounds weird. But people like people who resonate for them, who bring things together for them in some way. I've thought about it. Maybe it's because they remind them of something or someone, maybe even part of themselves. It's hard to explain. I guess it's hard to really ever know why you like someone."

And I'm thinking he's full of shit but I like him anyways.

"Look, Noah. I didn't even go to college. I don't even understand half the things you say to me."

"Yes you do."

"Don't say that. Maybe you want me to, but I don't." I can't stop myself. "But I do know I like you."

"So what's the problem?"

I look at him hard. I look at him with everything I got. "I'm supposed to get married. I mean, I have to get married." I take a breath. "I'm getting married."

"Oh."

"Yeah." He don't open his mouth. "You know what I'm saying?"

"I guess so."

We're like staring at each other.

Finally he speaks. "You're getting married only because you feel you have to, because of the baby."

"You got it."

He thinks for a minute. "Are you sure you have to?"

"You mean an abortion. I thought about it for maybe two minutes. No chance."

"No, actually, I didn't mean that. I mean, even with being pregnant, do you really have to?"

I think about Pop and Angie and Jeanette and Vinnie and even Ma who don't even know yet. "Oh, yeah," I tell him. "I have to."

He reaches over and takes my hand. "Look, Tina, just let me see you again. Keep seeing you. Okay?" He reaches in his pocket for a piece of paper. "Here. Write down your number."

"Noah, are you listening?"

"It's okay, Tina. Come on," he says, looking down at the empty snack bowls. "Let's get some supper."

Chapter 15

Turns out he's a regular guy. He takes me to some real classy place nearby but don't make a big deal about it. The restaurant's on the second floor, you wouldn't even know it was there. It's Italian, but not like no place I ever been. I mean, pizza isn't even on the menu. Noah orders this fancy meal with wine and all, stuff like *linguine con vongole* and *mozzarella in carrozza* and *frutta di mare*, but he's not showing off or nothing. That's what I mean. Some people, they can tell time, they think they're hot shit.

We sit there awhile, I'm looking around the restaurant. It's like somebody's house, the walls are brick and little tables all over with all kinds of people, old, young, like a family. There's one picture I keep staring at, these ladies in long white dresses at night, hanging up red and yellow Japanese lanterns. And they're looking at us like we surprised them. Like we came early to the party or something like that.

So we're talking a long time and I'm drinking the wine, taking tiny sips, and it's like he's a friend. I mean, except maybe for Tony I never could talk to a guy this way. Like I can tell him something and he don't laugh, or try to jump down my throat or look at me like I'm crazy. Like he knows I'm talking about me, not him, if you see what I mean.

So it don't seem wrong to let him take me home. I'm a fucking coward if you must know 'cause Vinnie's down at his sister's. Otherwise I would of said no. But I don't wanna leave this guy. He seems a little sad and then I start talking and he's happy. I don't know. Maybe I made it up.

He looks all around my place like he's a detective or something. "What, you lose something here?" I aks him.

He laughs. "No. Sorry. I'm just so curious about you." He's checking out the posters I brought home from the office. One lists safety rules for the clean room. Another one is of silicon, sliced like a salami. He don't know what to make of it.

"I just like 'em," I says. "I think they're funny, okay? Besides, they didn't cost nothing."

He thumbs through the *Glamour*s and starts up every one of my music boxes. Then he peeks into the kitchen. He's real nervous and I like him even better. I make coffee. Nick is wrong. I make real good coffee. Other stuff, too.

"Noah, look," I says. "I like you a lot. Usually, I wouldn't tell a guy right off. But let's just say the circumstances are a little weird. But you gotta swear to me that you're, well, healthy. You know?"

"Healthy?" He looks puzzled, then he blushes. "Oh, you mean that I'm not carrying anything."

"Yeah, and I don't mean luggage."

"Because of the baby."

"Because of the baby."

"Look, Tina, I can swear up and down but I can't prove it. Let me just tell you my situation. I was married for seven years. My wife and I broke up two months ago, although I guess you could say we hadn't been together for the last year. I haven't slept with anyone since."

"Did you fool around while you were married?"

He jerks his head back in surprise but answers anyway. "Once."

"Oh. And, uh, your wife? Did she fool around?"

"Adeena?" He laughs like he don't think it's funny. "No. I don't think so. I think it's pretty safe to give you a definite no on that one."

He sounds real put out and I wonder if she's queer or something.

"I didn't mean nothing."

"I'm not angry at you, Tina."

I tell you, a time like this, you gotta take your chances. I go over and start to kiss him. And he kisses back real hard and strokes my hair and moves his hand down my back and presses my body against his. Then we're undressing in the bedroom and he licks my whole body and puts his fingers inside me.

Then he takes me off the bed and we sit on the floor in front of the mirror on my closet door and he watches as he touches me all over. "You're beautiful," he tells me. He touches my belly. "The baby's beautiful."

I turn and start to lick him, watching myself in the mirror. He touches my breasts, my backside, then pulls me off and brings me down on top of him, and I move on him fast, faster it feels so good. He locks his legs around me to stop and then lets go and we both come strong and screaming.

After, I'm lying there on the floor, I can't believe it. He's kissing me and touching me so gentle and I want him again. We move to the bed and this time it's quiet, and afterwards we both sleep for a while. I wake up and wonder if Mrs. Gentile downstairs heard anything.

I stare at him while he's sleeping. Then I start to cry 'cause things are so mixed up. He wakes up and we just look at each other. Then I tell him he has to leave. "Anyone sees you, it'll be all over. They got big mouths here."

He starts to dress. His socks, his shoes, his goddamn underwear, I love.

Chapter 16

Jeanette calls in the morning all excited. She's had a great idea. We'll go to Kleinfeld's for my wedding gown. She'll call for the appointment. "And me and the bridesmaids can get our dresses there, too."

"Jeanette, you're crazy," I tell her straight out. "You sound just like Vinnie and I'll tell you what I told him. There ain't time for that. Besides, I'm not having no big wedding, get that through your head."

"Oh don't have some crummy little affair. You'll regret it, Teen." She breaks off to yell something at Donna. She comes back on. "You want something to remember your whole life."

"I don't think I'll forget it."

I hear her scream at Joey and aks Nick to take him. "So which church?"

"Which church what?"

"Which church you getting married in, dum-dum?"

"No church."

"Is that supposed to be a joke?"

"What are you giving me a hard time for, Jeannie? Who are you to start giving me this church business?"

"I think it's important. I go now for the kids."

"Bullshit. You go now for Nick's parents."

"That's not true, Tina."

"Yeah, right."

"Why must you always be such a little bitch?"

"Hey, I didn't call *you* up first thing in the morning to give you a hard time. You called *me*, remember?"

"Well excuse me."

"Fine. You're excused." But I'm not really angry. She don't hang up, neither.

"Jean?"

"What?"

"I'm gonna go tell Ma today."

"What you tell your mother is your business."

"What is this 'your mother' crap?"

"I don't talk to her since she tried to hurt Joey."

"She didn't try to hurt Joey. She wasn't strong enough to hold him is all. Come on, Jeannie, she don't know what she's doing half the time. She's not responsible."

"She knows what she's doing more than you think."

"Well, I gotta tell her."

"I'll tell you what you gotta do. You gotta start planning."

"Look, I'll call you later, let you know what happens, okay?"

"Whatever."

What the hell is everybody getting so mad about? I swear they treat me like some kind of little idiot. I'm not in such a great mood anymore, but I dial Grandma's number 'cause I gotta get this over with. She sounds surprised to hear from me.

"Tina, what made you remember you had a family? You in trouble or something?"

"No, Grandma, nothing's wrong. I just thought I'd come by later if it's all right."

"Why shouldn't it be all right? What? We have some place to go?"

"Ah, how's Ma?"

"How should she be? You'd know if you came more

often. But if you want to spend time with that bum of a father instead, that's your decision."

"Stop it, Grandma."

"Oh, I knew you'd take his part."

She's too much. No wonder Ma went crazy. "I'll see you in a little while, okay, Grandma?"

"If that's what you want."

Just as I'm leaving, the phone rings again and I'm hoping it's Noah. But it's Kathy, Pop's wife, and me and Vinnie should come for dinner tomorrow night. That's a laugh. She pretty much hates my guts, but I say yes because of Pop.

Then Vinnie calls. His sister's so happy and what about invitations and the band and she knows a photographer. Then Angie calls, do I wanna meet somewhere we'll go shopping and what about flowers?

Now I know why people get married. No one's paid so much fucking attention to me since I was five years old and got hit in the head with a swing and they took me to the Emergency.

Chapter 17

I'm scared about seeing Ma. Usually she don't look so good. Grandma tries to keep her up, but she dresses her in these old-lady clothes that don't fit. Last time I tried going shopping with her, though, she made a scene in the store like a little kid. Wouldn't try anything on. Then cursed out the salesgirl. I buy her stuff, but Grandma usually brings it back and gets her something cheaper. Then she has the nerve to tell me no more Macy's 'cause it's too much trouble to return things there.

They live all the way the hell downtown. It's Saturday, so most of the stores around here, the Jewish places, are closed. Funny little stores. You can't believe they make a dollar. I went into some once. They got stuff in cartons like it's crap or something. But you pick up a blouse it's fucking silk and a hundred bucks.

The streets are really filthy and graffiti all over. I don't think Grandma can see it no more and Ma don't care. I'm aksing myself what the hell I'm doing here. I'm just about the only white person around. All Spanish, you know? Like I said, I got nothing against nobody, but they sure don't make you feel welcome.

Ma and Grandma live in one of them project-type buildings that look old when they're new. You know, they build like ten of them together with some crummy little playground in the middle that gets destroyed in about three minutes.

Anyways, I think the two of 'em must get on each other's nerves in a one-bedroom. The rooms seem to get smaller each time I go up there. And the place stinks from cooking, like a window ain't been opened in forty years and you can smell all those burnt suppers of pot roast and hamburgers and lamb stew one on top of the other.

Grandma opens the door wearing this housedress with an apron over it. I guess I don't count as company. I kiss her, and she's already looking to see what I brought. Which today is just something from the bakery 'cause I didn't plan.

"Looks all right," she tells me, peeking inside the box. "But with my stomach, who can eat it?"

I leave the box on the kitchen table and go into the living room. Ma is sitting on the couch. She looks real thin and pale. I aks Grandma when's the last time she took her out.

"She don't wanna go out. You'll see."

I go over to Ma and try to kiss her, but she pulls back like I'm a stranger.

"It's Tina, Ma."

"I know who it is."

I see her eyebrows are penciled in kind of crooked and her lipstick is smeared. She's dyed her hair dead black. She looks like she's made up for Halloween.

"How you doing, Ma?" I sit down next to her. The couch is so lumpy it feels like I'm sitting on rocks. It's about four different shades of brown by now, and the threads have worn through in places on the back.

Ma turns to face me and gives me an angry look. "Did you bring me anything?"

"Sure, Ma. I brought some cake. Cannoli. You like 'em."

"Sure. She brings me guinea cake from that father of hers."

Now, I used to get upset about this shit she gives me

about Pop. But I'm used to it by now so I don't say nothing. Grandma's been poisoning her mind.

"I came to tell you something, Ma. I'm getting married."

"Ha! You hear that? She thinks she's getting married. Some wop, I bet. Watch out, you'll have bastards like I did."

Now Grandma puts her two cents in. "Who is it, Tina? That boy you been seeing? Yes? What's the matter with a Jewish boy? You girls never remember who you really are."

"Come on, Grandma, what does that matter now?"

"Sure, what do you care?" she says. "You never cared. You always made trouble for your mother. You was never good like your sister."

"Yeah," Ma pipes in. "You always had a big mouth, Tina." She shakes her head. "Not your sister."

"Jesus, Ma," I says, getting up. "I thought you'd be happy about this. Just forget it."

She keeps talking like she don't hear. "Your sister would never do anything to hurt me. She's not gonna throw her life away."

"Too late, Ma. You were there. She married Nick eight years ago. They got two kids."

"I don't know what you're talking about."

I go over to Grandma. "She's worse. How long she been like this?"

She shrugs. "She never had no trouble before she married your father."

"Pop took care of her! He still takes care of her!"

"Oh yeah? That why he divorced her? Look at her. That's how he took care of her."

I go kneel in front of Ma. "Grandma says you don't wanna go out no more. How come? You wanna go for a walk with me?"

"Can't go out."

"Why not?"

"They'll get me."

"Who'll get you?"

She looks around like she's afraid someone'll hear her. "The unions."

"The unions?"

"They're organizing. They're gonna take over."

"I won't let no one get you, Ma. I promise. Let's go out." I stand up and go to take her arm, but she pushes me away. She looks up to Grandma like she's scared.

"I told you!" Grandma says like she's glad or something.

I tell Ma I'm sorry. Then I wonder how Ma's been getting her medication if she won't go out to see the doctor like she's supposed to. "Grandma, is she getting the right treatment?"

Now she's really angry. "I do whatever gotta be done, thank you," she says.

I look around at the stained walls, the worn-out floor, the faded furniture. On the old TV is a tin vase with orange plastic flowers set on a plastic doily. I see the doily's turned gray with dirt. "Jesus, Grandma! Don't you never dust?"

"I do plenty," she tells me. She pushes past and yells back into the living room. "Tell her, Joan. Tell her what I made for supper last night."

"Last night?" Ma says like a little girl real proud she remembered something. "Last night we had meat loaf."

Grandma crosses her arms. "See? We're fine. That bum sends her a few dollars, I buy meat."

I can't take no more. "Okay, Grandma. I guess I'll go now."

"Go? You just got here!"

"I know, but I gotta meet somebody."

"Well, if that's more important."

"Come on, Grandma. Look, I'll let you know about the wedding. It'll probably be pretty soon."

Ma hears this. "Ha! I knew it. It better be pretty soon! You got yourself pregnant, didn't you, you guinea tramp!"

She starts to laugh hard and she's still laughing when I walk out the door.

On the corner, some guy with one arm is begging. He's wearing a sweat shirt with the sleeves torn so you can see his stump. I open up my wallet and give him every bit of change I got.

Chapter 18

I go uptown to meet Angie at Altman's. She's real nervous 'cause she never been there before. I think she feels like she don't belong or something, the store's too fancy, but I tell her you don't need no pass to get in. I mean, I never been here before neither, but I don't tell her that. I heard a couple of girls from *Skirt* on the elevator talking about it. "There are so few stores with real class left in New York," they says. So I like made a note of it, you know? Ange wants to go to Macy's, but I tell her I'm buying a wedding dress, I ain't buying no fry pan.

Inside, the place looks like it's turning yellow. Like paper does when it's been around too long. I don't know, maybe it's the light that's yellow, like they got a different kind of electricity. Maybe they save old light bulbs or something to make it look like that.

Anyways, we almost don't make it off the main floor what with looking at stuff: scarves and belts and gloves and hats and bags, and telling each other what we think. I love that. When you're with someone you can say, "Oh, look at those shoes. They're the ugliest pieces of crap I ever saw, and would you look at what they want for them!" And then you see this pocketbook or something that's so beautiful you could kill for it and it's really more than you wanted to spend but your friend says, "Oh, buy it if you really want it. You'll always be sorry if you don't."

Or you try on this dress and you can't tell if your butt is sticking out or if it's right for some affair you got to go to or something, and she says, "What? Are you kidding? It ain't no costume party." I mean, you go alone, you're only shopping, if you know what I mean.

We go up the escalator. It's real slow like you got nothing else to do all day. Or maybe so's they don't get all the old ladies too excited.

We get out at dresses. I think the stuff is a little frumpy, but I don't wanna let on to Ange. One or two nice things they got, but they're real pricey. We're going through the racks and nothing I pick she likes.

"Please, Teen. Can't you find something that's not black? This ain't stuff to get married in. Won't you even look at a gown? A real wedding gown?"

"I am looking at wedding gowns," I tell her. I hold up this navy blue suit. "You think I'd even be thinking of buying this thing if I wasn't getting married?" I show her the price tag. "It costs three hundred fucking dollars. What the hell else would I do in it but get married?"

Ange grabs a pleated pink chiffon and we go to try on. Two black salesgirls are in the dressing room talking their heads off, but they stop when we come in and smile and one of them hands us numbers. I look at Ange like, "See? They can be nice," but she don't notice. She don't see what she don't wanna see.

All the help is black now, except for the old-time sales-ladies. Those broads all seem to dress alike, in brown wool skirts that hang straight down with white blouses and glasses on chains around their necks and their hair in a bun. They look like they been here since the store opened.

I put on the suit and I look dead. You could say navy is not my color. Ange tries on her pink dress and looks great. It's low cut and has a wide belt with a rhinestone buckle.

It really sets her off. I tell her she should get the dress, but she says she's not sure Jim'll like it. So what, I says, but Ange looks at herself awhile and then takes it off.

"That suit needs a blouse, Teen. Something to liven it up. Stay here. I'll get you something."

I'm so tired I feel like I'm gonna drop, so by the time she comes back with an armful of bright red and yellow blouses with bows and ruffles, arguing with the salesgirls because she brought too many things into the fitting room, I'm struggling back into my jeans. They're real tight by now.

"Tina, what are you doing?"

"Sorry, Ange. I've had it. And I felt like an idiot standing there in that thing barefoot. You're right. It ain't for a wedding, and it don't look good, anyways."

She starts showing me the blouses. "This one's cute. Come on, Tina, try it on."

Then she sees my open jeans. "You already getting a little belly, huh?"

She says it so sweet I put on one of the blouses and slip the suit jacket over it. Ange smiles. "You look real smart, like some lady executive." Then she shakes her head. "But not no bride."

I rip off the outfit. "Let's please have something to eat."

So we leave all the stuff in the room and walk out past the girls, who give us dirty looks. We walk around the floor through the racks of clothes. Ange is still touching stuff, holding dresses up to show me. "They got nice things here, Teen. But the prices!"

"Well, Ange, they say you get what you pay for." She tilts her head and raises her eyebrows like maybe she didn't hear me right or something.

We go up to the restaurant they got up here in the store. I can tell Ange hates it, and to tell the truth, I don't blame her. I'm disappointed. I mean, get *real*, people. This place looks like the cafeteria in my old high school. Half the wall is phony brick and the other is painted with these dripping trees or something. And who's in here? The little old ladies wearing hats with veils and gloves and carrying canes. And who's resting on these round benches right outside? More of the same. Plus some poor old guy one of 'em dragged along.

And who decided to serve little white bread sandwiches all cut up? I mean, is that food? And get these waitresses with their little aprons! Shit. There's not one of 'em under fifty, I bet. They all have hair dyed orange and this real pale powder on, too. Makes 'em look like they ain't been outside for twenty years.

Ange is making a face at her food. She's right. It tastes like shit, but I'm so hungry I don't care. I can't stand this being hungry all the time. It's like something's taken over my body, like one of them extraterrestrials or something from a flying saucer in some dumb movie. I finish Ange's plate, too.

"Tina, I'm gonna throw up from this place. Look, I wanna go back to get that dress. I got my cousin's wedding next month and it'll be perfect. And then I can wear it to yours."

I shake my head. "It'll be too fancy, Ange. I'm not having no big affair. I wanna do it short and sweet. What's the quickest way?"

She laughs like I said something dirty.

"I mean to get married. Jeez."

She rolls her eyes. "City Hall."

"Yeah? You can really get married there?"

"Yeah. It takes about two seconds. You stand on a line like you're at the supermarket or something. I went through that with my Carla. You don't want that, Teen."

"No, that's just what I want. Sounds perfect."

She's almost crying. "That's it? That's all you want? You don't want a sit-down meal or nothing? Shit, Tina, don't you wanna be a bride?"

I feel bad. She cares so much. It makes me think about when I was eight years old or something like that and had this Ginny bride doll. God, was that the best. So I says, "I don't know, Ange. I guess a meal or something'd be okay. Yeah, sure. Lunch. That'll be good. We'll go to some restaurant afterwards or something." I like the idea. "Some real nice place. We'll get a guy in to take pictures. Don't worry, it'll be good."

I feel much better. I feel like I've planned the whole fucking wedding and can forget about it.

We pay for lunch and stop at the Ladies. They got this huge room just for sitting, and here are all the old ladies in their suits from the year one hanging out. It's like they came from another time warp or something, and like they're so cozy here after a hard day's shopping. It's okay, you know? Even with the old lady smell of crap and perfume.

We go back down to the dress department, and I'm waiting for Ange to try the dress on again, and I see this pale gray dress I know is perfect. It's got a drop waist so it won't be too tight around my belly. It hangs so soft. It's real silk and a shitload of money. I can see myself wearing pearls and carrying white roses. A salesgirl comes over and aks if she can help me. I tell her I want the dress in a six. Better make it an eight. No, I don't wanna try it on. I'll take it. And I'm thinking that Noah'll love it.

On the way home Ange is pissed she hasn't seen the dress, but I don't wanna show it to her 'cause I know she won't like it. And because I know she won't like it, I know I can't go and tell her about Noah.

But I'm feeling bad about being down on her so I go all the way to her house instead of getting off at my stop. I haven't been there for a long time because of Jim, but things seem to be quieter lately so I decide to take a chance.

He's not home when we get there and I'm glad. What is it with some guys? It's like it's their goddamn house and the wife is only visiting or something. Or the maid, more like it. Like she don't have the same rights. She gotta get permission.

We go into the bedroom and Ange is showing me these shoes she's got for the dress and some other stuff when we hear him come in. And all of a sudden, she gets nervous and I think, shit, how can you live like this? She just goes on showing me things and tries to ignore him like most girls would. I mean, after twenty years, you don't exactly run to the door.

At first he's quiet, but when she don't come out he calls for her. And she goes pronto. And then I hear her telling him I'm there and would he like to see the dress? And he gives her a hard time about it.

"You went and bought a dress without telling me? How much was it? I bet it was a lot. You bitch. What else haven't you been telling me?"

"Nothing, Jimmy. Please. Tina's here."

"I don't care who the fuck is here. I can talk in my own house and no fucking girlfriend of yours is gonna stop me."

"Look, I'll show you. I got the dress for Mary's wedding. I just thought . . ."

"You just thought. That's when you fucking get into trouble."

"I'll bring it back you don't like it."

"Do what you want. What the fuck makes you think I care? What the hell good is a new dress gonna do you? You're still gonna look like a witch."

"No, I'll make myself up real pretty. You'll see. You'll be real proud of me."

"That'll be the day."

"Ah, Jimmy, come on," she says, trying to sound all cutesy.

"Don't give me that 'Ah, Jimmy' crap."

His voice is real angry and I hear Angie gasp. I come out of the bedroom and he's got a hold of her arm and she's crying.

"Don't touch her, you bastard!"

He lets go and turns on me. "You get the hell outta here, you lousy bitch. You never come here again. You gotta hell of a nerve telling me what to do."

"Jimmy, please!" Ange cries. "Tina, just go. It'll be all right."

"Fucking A it'll be all right 'cause I'm calling the cops!"

He laughs. "The cops ain't gonna come because some fucking broad calls. What you gonna tell 'em? There's no law against a man talking to his wife."

"Is that what you call it?"

Ange pleads with me. "Tina, it's okay. He's just tired. Go home. I'll see you Monday."

"Yeah," Jim says. "I'm tired. I'm gonna go lie down. The show's over. Get outta here."

And I go, but I feel like a lump of shit, 'cause I know he's gonna let her have it soon as I'm gone. And I think —this must go on all the time. I mean, I used to think it was just every few months or so. But he went after her for nothing. So she must never know what's gonna set him off. Maybe it's just that every time he don't leave marks.

Chapter 19

Vinnie comes over, and he's pleased as a little kid when I tell him I got a dress. But he blows his stack at the City Hall deal.

"What the fuck way is that to start off? You gotta have a priest to make a wedding."

"When's the last time you were in church?"

"That don't matter. You gotta have religion when you get married."

"Okay. Let's get a rabbi then."

"What is that, a joke?"

"No one's laughing, Vinnie."

"Come on, Tina. You're Catholic and you know it."

"My mother's name was Schwartz, Vinnie."

"What's that supposed to mean?"

"It means if I'm Catholic, I'm Jewish, too. And it means I'm nothing and I'm not having no priest marry me."

"But some jerk-off clerk from City Hall can do it?"

I shrug. "I'm a New Yorker."

"You're a ball breaker, that's what you are, Tina." But he don't sound angry.

"It'll be nice, Vin. We'll invite a few people and then

take 'em out to lunch. We'll have a photographer. It'll be real classy, you'll see."

"I guess, Teen. I just thought it'd be a big blow-out. You know."

"You wanna wait till I'm eight months pregnant and marry a big white blimp? That'd be a hell of a church wedding."

He smiles. "I suppose. But I thought girls wanted that sort of thing."

"You marrying some girl or you marrying me, Vinnie?"

"Now don't get all excited, Tina. We'll do it your way. Just take it easy. I don't want the baby to pop out early or nothing."

Jesus, he gets me crazy. But I don't say nothing, I just fix my face 'cause we're going to the Mt. Etna, which is his favorite place to eat. We can sit and talk about who to invite, Vinnie says. Some shit like that. Fine. Whatever.

The place is a hole in the wall practically in the stinking Gowanus Canal, so don't aks me why there's a line, even if it is a Saturday night. I mean, I guess I used to think the food was pretty good, too. There's a group of black people waiting for a table and Vinnie says something like, "Not the usual crowd," kind of annoyed.

"They got a right to be here, too, Vinnie."

"Come on, Tina. They had to come all the way over here to eat? They don't have no restaurants where they come from?"

"So what's it matter to you?"

"It don't matter nothing to me. But it's a neighborhood place. People like to see neighborhood people here."

"Maybe they are neighborhood people. I don't know. Maybe the place got written up in some newspaper or something. Maybe they know the fucking chef."

"Very funny."

"Jesus, Vinnie, what the hell's so terrible?"

"You just don't understand things, Tina."

I'm gonna answer him back, but one of the black guys

just then goes over to Tom Empedocles, the owner, and aks about his table. The guy's getting real angry, I can see. I bet they been here awhile.

Tom says something and shrugs and the guy raises his voice and says something like, "Are you saying you're not going to serve us?" And then Tom says something real loud about reservations. Then the guy's friends try to get him to leave but he won't budge.

There's a couple of women with them and they look worried. They're like backing themselves toward the door. Now Tom and the guy are really yelling at each other and two or three waiters come around and one of them says, "Hey, I think it's time you left," and kind of shoves the guy, and the guy starts to take a swing, but his friends pull him back and then everybody's screaming and the black guys are being pushed out and the women, too, and we all watch as they stand outside still yelling and Tom yells out he's gonna get a cop and the guy's friends drag him off to their car.

Everybody inside is standing around congratulating themselves with these big grins on their faces. "Did you see that guy?" one of the waiters is aksing. "What an ape!"

Vinnie laughs. I can't believe it. I wanna go. When Tom comes over to seat us I aks him what the problem was. "They just wanted to eat," I says.

Vinnie looks at me like I'm crazy. "Don't pay no attention to her," he tells Tom.

Tom puts up his hands like everything's okay with him. He's a nice guy, you see. "I know. The young people got different ideas."

We sit but I'm furious. "I don't wanna eat here, Vinnie. I don't wanna give this guy my money."

"First of all, shut up. Second of all, it's my money."

"I'll give you shut up. Don't tell me to shut up."

"Tina, what the hell is wrong with you? Since when have you been so in love with the colored?"

"Oh, forget it, Vinnie."

"You're right, I'll forget it. I'm not saying they don't

deserve a fair shake. I'm just saying they should stay away from where they're not wanted. What the hell were they doing here? There must of been something to it."

"Whaddaya mean?"

"I mean what the hell did they come here for? They must of come all the way from Bed-Stuy. What the hell they want with Italian food? Don't they eat fried chicken and shit? Now let's get off it, Tina. I can't believe you're making such a thing about it."

But I can't stop. "You never ate fried chicken in your life, right?"

"What the hell does that matter?"

"It matters that you're stupid, okay, Vinnie? That you don't even know what you're talking about half the time."

Now he's good and mad. He grabs my arm across the table and talks low and angry. "Don't you ever call me stupid. What the fuck gives you the right? You care more about those colored than about me? You're fucked up, you know that, Tina? You better straighten yourself out and fast."

And suddenly I don't care anymore. What do I care what Vinnie thinks about anything? He's a guy I know. He's an okay guy. "I'm sorry, Vinnie. I just didn't like it, is all."

He lets out a breath and takes away his hand. Now he's happy again. "Sure, sure. I know, being pregnant makes you all emotional. I read something about it somewheres." He smiles like I should be real proud of him.

"That's it, Vin."

So we eat.

Chapter 20

Kathy's running in and out of the kitchen like she's cooking some big-deal dinner she can't leave for two minutes. Not that she's a bad cook or nothing, but not that great. Don't aks me why Pop's gained all that weight.

They been married for two years now, and I guess he's happy enough. She's about fifteen years younger than him and don't have no kids and I don't know what the story is, whether she wants them or what. Maybe she messed herself up inside from all the drinking, although she's been straight since she met Pop. Jeanette keeps predicting she's pregnant. "Oh, yeah, just wait," she says, like it'd be the worst thing that ever happened. "Pop'll tell us any day now." But so far, no go.

Vinnie and Pop are sitting in the living room watching the game, so they don't need to talk too much. God. Football. There's a new TV and almost all new furniture. I can see she likes pretty stuff. I bet she couldn't wait to get rid of anything of Ma's. But I guess they got the dollar, what with them both working. She was married before, too, so I guess some of the stuff was hers.

Her first husband was a real bum. She got lucky with

Pop. She was working part-time at the laundromat and Pop brought in his clothes and they got to talking, I guess. She's got real white skin and in the summer gets freckles all over. Pop calls her Freckle. He thinks that's cute. I guess she's Irish or something. She's got little eyes and a little nose. Don't aks me what he sees in her.

But she seems real happy about my wedding, I'll give her that, and when I offer to help with bringing out the food she says, "No. You're a bride. You don't gotta do that. Sit down. You'll never have it so good again." I just hope that ain't a crack about Pop, is all. She better watch it.

So she's running back and forth, checking the sauce, the pasta, so's I can hardly say a word to her and finally I yell, "Kathy, slow down. Nobody's even that hungry." And she kind of laughs this little laugh.

And suddenly I see it's not that she don't like me. It's just that she's nervous. I make her nervous. Which is a joke, considering how she took Pop away and all.

When we sit down the bell rings and it's Aunt Vicky. She's got the worst timing of anyone I ever met. I mean, Vinnie and me'll be in the middle of making love and it's Aunt Vicky on the phone. When Jeanette and me was kids, she'd decide it was time to come over and clean at night when Pop was trying to get us to bed. So of course Kathy kills herself making this meal and we haven't had one bite and Aunt Vicky comes in and looks hurt how come no one invited her?

"Something special going on?"

"What special, Vicky?" Pop aks. "We're eating Sunday dinner. Sit down. Kathy made meatballs."

Aunt Vicky looks them over like maybe it wouldn't kill her but she's not gonna exactly enjoy it, either.

"So, Tina. Anything new?"

"Yeah, Aunt Vicky. Vinnie and me are getting married."

She don't look at me, she looks at Pop. "Oh, that's so nice. If someone had told me maybe I would of known."

Pop shakes his head. "It just happened a few days ago, Vicky. The kids haven't told hardly anybody, right?"

"I told my family, of course," Vinnie says.

"Of course *you* told *your* family, Vinnie," Aunt Vicky says with this sick smile.

"Jesus, Aunt Vicky, we're gonna invite you," I tell her. "Besides, it ain't gonna be a big deal."

"My niece getting married and nobody tells me. That's a big deal to me."

Kathy is pressing her hands together and looking at all the food. "How about some salad, Vicky?"

"Maybe just a little," she says, smiling like she's having a good time trying to decide who to hit first. I roll my eyes at Pop. Christ. She's a bigger pain in the ass than she used to be. No wonder Pop got married again. I mean, I know why. He's still young. Not that we ever talked about it. I mean, you don't talk about stuff like that with your father. But he must of also done it to get away from Aunt Vicky. I mean, what with Nonna and Papa dead, she decided to adopt Pop. I guess being married to Ma was pretty bad, but being looked after by Vicky was worse.

So she listens to what I'm saying about the wedding plans like she's real interested but she's gonna have to excuse herself and go throw up.

"I see, yes. No. No, I never heard of that restaurant. Well, if you say it's nice, Tina. Of course, maybe if you'd said something, someone could of helped you plan this thing. No, I'm not saying nothing. I'm sure it'll be very nice."

Actually, I can tell Pop's not too thrilled neither, but what can I do? What I'm really waiting for is my stomach to pop and Aunt Vicky's eyes'll pop too. She thinks she's mad she didn't know about the wedding. Wait'll she finds out I'm pregnant.

We finish, and Kathy don't want help clearing up, but Vicky starts taking things from the table and stacking them up in the kitchen. "Really, Vicky, I got my own method of doing things. Just sit down." But Vicky acts like she don't hear and Kathy gives up.

Vicky leaves before dessert. "I don't wanna put you out," she tells Kathy. When she's gone, like an emptiness is in the room. I mean, none of us likes Vicky—we love her of course—but for once we don't want her to go. The football game's over, so Pop and Vinnie play cards. Me and Kathy are stuck with each other again and I'm in a bad mood.

I mean, I know Vinnie's still disappointed about the wedding, and now Pop and Kathy are too. Jeannie, everybody. I bet Donna's mad at me for godsake. Shit. I can't do nothing right. I sit there in the kitchen stewing while I'm watching Kathy do the dishes. She's got one of them double-sided sinks. First she rinses the dishes on one side. Then she soaks 'em in soapy water on the other. Then when the soapy side's full she takes them back out and washes them off on the other side. I can't believe I'm seeing this.

Anyways, while I'm watching this I have a bright idea. "Hey, Kathy, what about if you and Jeannie'll be my brides-maids?"

She looks up. "You mean matrons of honor?"

"Whatever."

"Great. Sure. I'd like that, Tina, if you're sure and all. I mean, if you don't think Jeannie'll mind."

"Why should she mind?"

"Well, you're sisters and all. And besides, what about your mother?"

I feel like a jerk. "I hadn't thought of that. Shit, I was just trying to make people look forward to this thing."

"Oh, Tina, everybody's looking forward. Look, I don't need to be no bridesmaid."

"Okay, Kathy. But I'll get you flowers or something."

"That'll be real nice." She goes back to rinsing off the tomato sauce and I figure she's thinking about something else but after a while she says, "How about this? How about if you had Donna be your flower girl?"

She's really smart. I love that idea—Donna in a pretty dress throwing rose petals over everything. So I go in and tell Pop and Vinnie and they think that's a good thing, and I go to call Jeannie, but Nick answers but still I feel better. Then Donna gets on and I can tell she don't quite understand about it but likes it anyways, and I feel good. I feel like for once I been a good girl.

Chapter 21

The next day Angie don't show for work and I know something's up. I call her soon's I get a chance and she tells me she's sick. "Don't give me that," I says. "I was there, remember?" But she don't wanna admit it. What she's really upset about is that Dominick, her youngest, is moving out to live with Carla, his sister. She's right nearby so he don't gotta change schools or nothing. "Ange," I says, "if nothing was wrong why would Dommy be moving out?" But she don't answer.

I gotta get off 'cause Lynn is nosing around and it's none of his beeswax. He hands me all these tables and charts and shit 'cause we're doing this special test-and-measurement trade-show issue, and Tony's running around giving everybody new assignments. I hear Gene, the crybaby, complaining about how the hell is he supposed to do another story on top of all the stuff he's gotta handle all by himself, not like other people with some decent backup in the field, for godsake? Tony talks to him real nice like he really cares or something, but I know it's bullshit. Except Gene can't see it, the jerk. No one can stand Gene, except Lynn, of course. Two of a kind.

So I'm sitting with the work piled up to there and meanwhile, of course, the phone's ringing off the hook 'cause all the flacks in the goddamn industry just gotta be sure we got their fucking press releases first thing Monday morning, and every jerk-off doing research has all these dumbass questions they just gotta aks this minute, and I'm the one that's gotta try and answer 'em 'cause suddenly everybody's too busy to pick up their friggin' extension. And frankly, I'm glad, 'cause it's the kind of day takes your mind off yourself, if you know what I mean.

Fern calls up 'cause she don't want Lynn seeing her come by to aks me for lunch. I mean, even with what she told me, I wasn't looking to make a big deal of our relationship. But I'm glad she aksed 'cause I need to talk to someone.

We go to the Colonial Kettle, which is for shit, but the other coffee shop's been closed by the Board of Health. When we get there, I see it's *her* needs to talk. "Tina," she says, "I know you've got a lot to deal with right now, to say the least, but I hope you don't mind listening to me a minute."

So what can I say? And then she's telling me about her affair with Dave. I'm sitting here, it's like my hair and clothes are picking up the smell of her story along with the smell of the grease. Like I'm afraid when we go back to the office everyone's gonna know just from looking at me. I'm wondering why *she* don't mind, but then I tell myself I'm going too far. It's just that, you know, it makes me uncomfortable.

"I mean, he's sweet, Tina. Not a strong-arm type. Real vulnerable. But sexy, don't you think?"

I don't wanna hear this shit. It's none of my business. "To tell you the truth, Fern, I never thought about it. But he's cute, I guess. Look, Fern, you don't want me to think of him that way. I'm gonna be his secretary."

"Oh, Tina," she says, like she's tired of talking about it, too. She starts to play with the sugar packets on the table, taking them out of the little bowl and arranging them in piles. State flowers or sailboats, or some crap like that. Always something never in a million years would you be interested in seeing a picture of.

The food comes. All the coffee shops around here are Greek. They give you a lot of whatever, and drown it in tomato sauce. Fern can't eat. I take her salad. Feta cheese, Jesus, a big fat square of it. Who's idea was that?

So she's gonna quit because she can't stand Lynn and Dave's driving her crazy: Is he, isn't he, gonna leave his wife? She's fed up with these computer guys anyhow. They still think it's cute when a woman comes to interview them and they make a big point of explaining what a microchip is, like she thinks it's something you serve midgets at parties or put into small cookies. Then they're always flirting with her. And she's not even that great looking. I mean, not to be a bitch or anything. She's okay, I guess. Maybe if she got contacts.

"Fern," I says, "forget about him. He'll never be able to make up his mind to leave his wife. Maybe *she'll* leave *him*, but you can't wait around for that."

"How can you know, Tina?"

"Shit, Fern, just look at the way he is at work. You think this guy's gonna go out on a limb?"

She laughs. "Well, if he's pushed."

"You push him, he falls off."

She sits back in the booth nodding. And I'm right. I don't know how I know I'm right, but I am. Maybe I should be leading her life. I sure fucked up mine.

I'm gonna aks her how come she don't go out with Tony, but figure that's really none of my business, so now I tell her about the wedding and, what the hell, aks her to come. Me and Vinnie picked a Tuesday at the end of the month. He wanted Friday, but I knew no one from the office would go on a Friday because of deadline. He's right, though. No one gets married on a Tuesday. What the hell kind of day is Tuesday to get married?

"So you've called it off with that guy?" she's aksing me.

"What guy?" Like I don't know what she's talking about.

"You know, Tina, the guy with the business card."

"I don't know. I seen him Friday, but he hasn't called since then."

"It's only Monday."

"Yeah, well, I don't have time for bullshit."

"Do you like him?"

"I like him."

"A lot?"

"A lot."

"So what are you going to do?"

"Pray he calls, 'cause I gotta see him again."

"You're blushing."

"Well, you would too if you was thinking about what I'm thinking about."

"Did you sleep with him?" Her eyes couldn't get any wider.

"Oh yeah."

She shakes her head. "Tina, think about what you're saying. In one breath you invite me to your wedding, in the next you're telling me how hot you are for this guy. Look, lots of women have babies and don't get married."

"Not where I come from."

"So what?"

"It would be hard on my family."

"They'll get over it."

"How would I live?"

"Dave'll keep your job for you."

"And who'll watch the baby?"

"You'll find someone."

"Just like that."

"No, not just like that. I'm just saying it can be done."

"You mean tell Vinnie the wedding's off?"

"If that's what you want."

"I better do that pretty quick."

"I think so."

"But what if Noah never calls me again? I'll feel like a dope."

"Look, Tina, you want to marry Vinnie, marry him, you

don't, don't. If this Noah doesn't pan out, maybe someone else will. Or maybe you'll never marry. And, frankly, it'll be harder to find someone with a kid."

"Thanks a lot."

"You know what I'm saying."

"You're saying I can be chickenshit and do the easy thing or stick my neck out and maybe get hurt."

"Or be chickenshit and maybe get hurt."

"Yeah."

The waitress comes over and I'm embarrassed 'cause all the plates are on my side. Well, so what. Chicken's good for you. And rice. And those canned green beans.

When we get back there's a message for me. Of course it has to be Frieda that took it. "Some guy, Tina, but he wouldn't leave his name." She smiles and hangs around like she's waiting for me to tell her something. Let her wait all day.

I recognize the number. It's Noah. I wish Lynn would disappear off the face of the earth so I could call right now. I stuff my bag in my desk drawer and tell him I'm gonna check the fax and go quick before he can say anything. I take the stairs to the lunchroom and get into the phone booth and dial. My head is pounding by the time Noah gets on. He says hello and I'm like having a heart attack. Everything's bunched up inside me till it hurts. I know my voice sounds funny. It's like I forgot how to talk.

"Hi, it's Tina."

"Hi. I want to see you."

"Me too."

"I was away this weekend. That's why I didn't call."

"That's okay. I mean, you should of said."

"From now on."

"We really gotta talk."

"Would you come to my place after work? I'll make you supper."

"Sure. Why not?"

I mean, I didn't say hardly anything, but I have to sit

there and take a deep breath before I can get up. Some guy from the mailroom is standing outside the booth looking at me like when am I gonna get out of there? Fucking too bad.

Marv is by the fax when I get there, trying to send something and getting pissed 'cause it don't go through. "How's your girlfriend?" he aks me, meaning Angie, 'cause she's the one usually does that for him. But he don't aks like he cares she's sick or something, more like he knows she's fooling and she told me and I'm covering up for her. These fucking guys. Like they can do what they want and we're out sick we're faking. This Marv's not even that bad a boss, but you gotta watch his hands. You stand around at a meeting, he'll come right up behind and brush against you, then say excuse me like it was a accident or something.

Lynn's talking to some PR guys from DEC when I get back and they go into the conference room, so I call up the restaurant and aks about the wedding. It's the place Noah took me. I don't know any other place as nice. Besides, it's Italian, which'll make everyone but Ma and Grandma happy. Jesus, I can just see them there.

Why people have to work till five I'll never know. Why can't you just say, hey, it's slow right now, I'm going out for a walk? Or, I think I'll leave early today because I feel like it? I mean, if you do your job, why not? But nobody does it. They stick it out like little kids who can't do nothing unless they're told.

By three I'm so tired I can hardly keep my eyes open. I don't realize what it is right away. It's funny how you can forget about big things like being pregnant. I mean, I guess that's how people get by. They don't put out the upsetting things in life right in front of them, like a photo you place on your desk to look at all the time, or something important on your calendar you scribble stars and arrows on to remind yourself about. It's more like they bury 'em under the mail and the typing paper and whatever they're doing and every now and then they work through to the bottom of the pile and say, "Oh, yeah, that, I almost forgot about that."

I'm worried Lynn'll notice about me and put two and two together because the pig has like six kids or something, too bad for them, but he don't seem to see anything wrong. Tony sees, though, and aks do I wanna leave early. He's real upset, but the last thing I need is to have everybody aksing how come Tina gets to go home?

But I'm grateful. I mean, most guys are just so out of it. I always wonder when you read about these bigamists, how they had two wives in different places, two houses, two sets of kids and like the wives don't know nothing about it for years. That don't make no sense to me. How could a woman not know something was up? But a woman could have two husbands, I bet, and the slobs would never, never catch on. She could put 'em in the same room, they'd never figure it out.

Rochelle comes by to chat. She always does that when Angie's out, like she's been waiting to make her move. She tries to play up to people, but I see right through her. Always one of the girls with me and Ange, Miss Sophisticate with Fern, and then a hot number with the guys. Like she don't know who she is. They hired her as a copy editor, but she stinks. She's always spending time on the wrong things and telling people how to write their stories, then misses about half the typos.

I give Ange a call and she says she's fine. I tell her I'm gonna go to the police. She tells me I better not. "What is with you, Angie? I really can't stand this no more. Why won't you do nothing about it? Haven't you had enough?" It's just the way he is, she says, what can she do? Everybody got their problems. "You're gonna have a problem," I tell her. "If you're out too many days you'll lose your job." Don't aks me why I said that, unless it was to scare her. Jesus, what would it take?

Chapter 22

Noah's already there when I get to his place so I know he must of taken off early. You wouldn't believe his apartment, but what good is it way the hell up here? I'd never live on the West Side. They got a million stores and restaurants, but it's worse than downtown. Too many people, too much going on, and too much crime.

I can't help telling him how nice his place is, though. I mean, you should see it. So pretty. So big.

"This place is huge! You live here alone?"

"I used to share it with my wife, but she bought a co-op in the Village."

Shit. They must be swimming in money. I poke around while he's in the kitchen putting stuff in these big pots. It's like a kitchen in a magazine, with black and white tiles all over the walls. I go to the living room. There's so much to look at here, that's what hits me. The colors of the furniture, gray and pink and yellow and like a green-blue. Stripes on some things, flowers on others. Even the walls are some darkish red. Kind of a blood color, really, but nice. And there are rugs everywhere with different designs, and pillows on the sofas and chairs, and paintings on the walls and these colored boxes on the tables and candlesticks and vases full of flowers. I never seen anything like it. Like all his stuff is out. Or like there are a few layers. Most people, it's like they have just one layer in their houses and everything is separate from everything else. But here, there's stuff on top of stuff and things like mix into each other. It's better than Altman's, or Madison Avenue or the museum.

"Did you do this yourself?" I call into the kitchen.

"What, the mess?"

"No, this place, fix up all of this?"

"I did it with Adeena. My, uh, wife."

"What's she like?"

"There's a picture of her on the mantel."

I go over and see some snaps of him with this tall, thin woman. I look twice because the woman looks black. Real light, but definitely black. I take one of the pictures into the kitchen.

"This her?"

"Yeah. The beautiful Adeena."

"She's black, right?"

He laughs. "Right. Find that strange?"

"I guess so."

"Well, it was at first for me, too."

"She a model or something?"

"Yeah. Well, an actress, I guess. She's been in some commercials."

"Really?"

"Uh-huh. It's no big deal. Maybe you saw her. She played a branch manager in some bank spots. She smiled helpfully and wore a suit. And she was a stewardess on a soap episode." He makes his voice real high and perky. "We'll be landing in Dallas shortly." He laughs. "Anyway, she's got her hopes, heaven knows."

"She any good?"

"She's okay. She certainly thinks very well of herself."

All the time he's chopping up onions and mushrooms and other stuff and cooking spaghetti and running the blender. I mean, I'm used to sitting around Jeanette's kitchen, or Kathy's even, but not no guy's.

"I never had a guy cook me a meal in my whole life. Even when it was just Pop and us girls, Aunt Vicky'd bring stuff over."

"Did your mother ever cook?"

"Uh, I don't know. I don't remember." I feel like I'm getting a headache or something.

"Don't you ever talk about it, Tina? About your mother?"

"Yeah, of course. Why shouldn't I?"

"Sorry. It's just that you seemed really uncomfortable when I brought it up." He carries a pot over to the sink.

I take a deep breath. "How about Adeena? Didn't she cook?"

"Adeena? Not much. No, that sort of thing wasn't for her."

"Well, I guess there's no law she had to cook."

He looks up at me over the steam from the spaghetti. "No. No law. But some interest in normal human activity would have been a nice touch."

"Look, you married her. You must of known what she was like, so don't go blaming her."

"Hey, save it," he says, opening a bottle of wine. "She doesn't need any advocates. And I'm not such a bad guy, remember? It's just that I thought, you know, you get married and everyone pitches in. Makes a life together. Adeena and I were off and running in different directions from the opening bell."

I wave away the wine and he pours me some fancy seltzer and sticks a slice of lemon in it. I sit there watching the lemon float in the bubbles and listening to him talk. He talks like the living room looks. I'm not even listening to the words so much as just the sound of them, but suddenly I feel like I've figured something out.

"So she didn't want kids."

He makes a face and nods. "She didn't want kids."

So here I am in this gorgeous place with this guy I'm crazy about and if I could make it his kid inside of me by wishing I would in a minute.

"It's funny how things turn out," is all I can think of to say. What a jerk.

We're sitting eating the pasta with shrimp and stuff in it and he's so cute 'cause he's happy I like it, when we hear the door open. Noah sits back and listens like he don't know what's going on. Then he like smiles and gets up. I follow him. There's his wife with a shopping bag from Henri Bendel. She tosses it on the couch like she don't give a shit. She's one of those people who don't look quite real, you know? She's tall, her face is shining, her makeup, hair, are perfect. She's wearing this long black dress that flows down to her ankles and these woven white sandals with little heels. She's like a goddamn queen.

When she sees Noah she smiles, but she's not looking at him but behind him, giving me a real going-over. Then she tightens her lips like she don't like what she sees.

"Well," she says. "You certainly didn't waste any time."

He don't say nothing about that.

"I thought you didn't keep a key, Adeena."

"Oh, come on, Noah. You know I left things here. Isn't it easier for me just to pop in when I have to than to bother you all the time?"

"That's just like you, Adeena. So considerate."

"Oh, Noah, you're a real drag, you know that?"

She goes into the bedroom. Noah goes after her. He's nervous. It's like he's angry at her but glad to see her, you know? I mean, who wouldn't be glad to see her? But I can tell she's someone always makes you feel like you said the wrong thing.

I stay in the hall and watch her throw some stuff into a duffel bag. Then she walks out of the room holding up this green dress and comes over to me. "Here, honey. This is too small on me. You're little, you take it."

I'm too surprised to open my mouth. But Noah's mad as hell.

"She's not the goddamned maid, Adeena. She doesn't need your castoffs."

"Oh grow up, Noie. It's a nice dress and I can't wear it. Your little miss can use it, judging by the looks of things."

She turns back to me. "No insult, hon. It takes money to get the right clothes, don't I know it?" She goes over to the couch and lifts the outfit she just bought out of the Bendel's bag and holds it up. It's a red suit with a fitted jacket and short, straight skirt, and even on the other side of the apartment I can tell how soft the wool is.

She stuffs it back in, stands up and sniffs. "You've been cooking, right, Noie? How sweet. Well, she *is* pretty. But that hair!" She gives him this peck on the cheek and heads for the door. She touches the ends of my hair as she passes. "Get it cut," she says, and goes out.

Noah picks up a plate from the table and carries it into the kitchen like he forgot we were in the middle of eating. I don't say nothing, 'cause I see he's real upset. He says he's sorry about Adeena and all, but I tell him never mind. I was too interested in looking at her to care what she said.

Except that I see how things really are. "You still love her," I tell him. I'm not mad or nothing. Just a little sad. He comes over and holds me and we walk into the bedroom. What the fuck, right? I see she's pulled stuff out from everywhere and the place is a mess.

When he touches me, I can hardly catch my breath. He strokes my arms, presses my hands. I kiss him hard, bite him. He pulls me close. He says he loves my hair. Nobody has long hair anymore, he says. He twists it in his hands and tugs it. He's kissing me all over. He pushes up my dress, pulls down my panty hose and underpants. He reaches inside me while he's licking me and holds me down with his other arm. I want him inside me but he keeps licking me until I don't care and I come and then he jams into me hard and stops himself and then moves quicker and quicker and I come again and then he comes hard, shaking. He plays with my hair. All he says is, "Don't marry this guy."

I sleep for a while and then get up to leave. But he wants me to stay. "Please," he says, getting out of bed and picking up the green dress. "What the hell? Why not wear it tomorrow?"

I shake my head. "I can't wear your wife's stuff."

"Why not? She said you could have it."

"I don't want her dress."

He goes to the closet and starts picking through everything, holding things up. "You don't like it? Choose something else." He throws some outfits on the bed. "Look, Tina, this is the stuff she left behind. This is stuff she'd never remember she had in a million years."

"She'd remember. Women remember their clothes."

But I can't help it. I go over to the closet. The stuff is beautiful. Evening dresses and shoes and bags, and sweaters neatly folded in stacks on the shelves. It's like a dream wardrobe like maybe you could afford for your doll but never in your whole life for yourself. Noah lies on the bed watching while I look through everything, hold it up. I go through the drawers. She's got unopened panty hose. I mean by the dozens. Slips, bras, underpants, nightgowns. All silk. I can't believe it.

But I feel cheap. I feel like a thief. Here I am fucking her husband and touching her clothes. "I better leave," I tell him.

"Okay, Tina. You're right. You don't need her old clothes. We'll get you all new things."

"It's not that, Noah. You don't have to get me nothing."

"I'd like to."

I have to laugh. "Yeah? I'm not gonna be able to wear no nice clothes for a while."

His face lights up. "Hey. That's it. Please, Tina, let me do that, let me buy you the most beautiful maternity clothes in the whole goddamned world."

"Noah, I'm gonna marry somebody else in less than four weeks."

"Maybe."

"Probably."

"Let me do it anyway."

I make a face. "Okay. It'll be your wedding present."

"Great. Does that mean I'm invited?"

"Jesus, don't you think it would be a little weird?"

"Why? I'm a friend."

"I don't fuck my friends." I can see he don't like that.

"That was putting it a little crudely."

"Look, you don't like the way I talk, you don't like the way I am? That's tough shit. I told you how things were right off. Look, I don't need you, okay? You're messing up everything. Don't go playing games with me. I'm in no position for that. You like the body? Well, the mouth comes along with it."

Now I'm crying and he's holding me. "I'm sorry. I didn't mean it like that, okay? You're right. I'm playing a game. Just don't cut me loose yet."

He walks me outside and puts me in a cab, but I don't let him give me the money even though it's gotta be fifteen bucks from way the hell up here back to Brooklyn.

The cab moves slowly into the darkness. We get into a rhythm and catch all the lights for ten blocks. The buildings here are tall and old and look over the park. I feel protected in the cab and sit with my bag on my lap not moving, just looking out the window. The driver pulls onto the West Side drive. It's then I see that the city is on the water. I mean, I know that, but whenever you see the docks, you really know it. Here everything is about the boats that come in or used to come in bringing important stuff that guys unloaded, cursing and sweating. I mean, it's ugly here, in a way. Warehouses and the highway half-fallen down, riding between the pillars, the high wire fences, the meat district set back a little ways and then the other meat market—the guys hanging out on the rotting piers. And then we turn and go across Canal into Chinatown, always a million people no matter what the hour, stands still set up selling vegetables and fish, and we get to the river and can see the Brooklyn Bridge so pretty so pretty it is with its little pearls of light and the new pier below all lit up like a carnival. And then the excitement falls away and I'm home, everything familiar, quiet, but I feel I'm still shining, I'm a light on the bridge, I'm taking it with me. It's the baby, it's Noah, it's this feeling I have.

Part
II

Part
II

Chapter 23

I'm laughing. The new guy just knew something no one else did, not even Lynn, about some honcho's been fired at Hewlett-Packard, and Lynn's trying to be cool. I mean, Dave made him hire this guy and I know he would of quit sooner than do it except where the hell else is he gonna go? What the hell else does he know?

Dave, the wimp, would of let him get away without hiring no minorities, too, except we just got bought up and the place that bought us just had this big discrimination suit, and they sent around people to check out who was working at all the papers and guess what? You never saw so many black faces around here coming in for interviews.

So finally Lynn hires Yoshi and it's really pretty funny 'cause the guy's half-Japanese and half-black. Yoshi Brown. Except soon nobody's gonna remember his name 'cause they're all calling him Brothersan. And already some of the guys are making crudo jokes about how one half of his brain cancels out the other. But I tell you, he's real cute, and I'm not the only one who thinks so. Don't tell me it's a coincidence that he starts working here and two days later Fern comes back from lunch with contact lenses.

"Oh I've been meaning to do it for a while," she says all innocent. Cut the crap, I'm thinking. The guy's a hunk.

He's nice too, sort of, and smart. Lynn's trying to freeze him out, but I don't think he can afford to for long. He made him work with Gene, and Gene's been hopping mad ever since. Gene don't like no one to show him up and he's been giving Yoshi all the crap stuff like gallium arsenide to write about. It's hard to believe, really. I mean, here's a guy they could send out to Nikon or Toshiba or Kyocera. But people like Lynn got their brains so twisted they can't see what they're looking at.

I can't even be bothered with that shit, if you must know, 'cause I'm gonna have this baby, and I got more on my mind than DRAMs and disk drives and EpROMs and steppers and LANs. I mean, basically, I guess I'm happy. Except sometimes I feel like I'm in some kind of fucked-up kid's game, with me running away from Vinnie and Noah running away from me. But it's funny, even with things looking a little shaky with Noah, it don't make me wanna run to Vinnie and get tagged.

It's weird not having Vinnie around, though. I mean, I know I treat him like dirt, but it wasn't so bad spending time with him. I guess I even miss him now since Noah's always so busy all the time. It makes me a little worried. I call, he's away, he's in a meeting, he's traveling. Or maybe that's just what that little dirtbag receptionist is telling me.

I guess I'm kind of lonely. I must be, 'cause I even had dinner with Rochelle one night. I can tell she decided that it'll make her look good to be my friend. Fine. When my baby's here, I'll drop her like wrapped dog shit. Meanwhile, she'll do, with Ange out again. I mean, she just got back after the last time. This time she says it's pneumonia.

I can't believe her, the way she can't stand up for herself. You gotta take things in hand, not wait around your whole life. So I'm through talking this marriage business over with people. I gotta tell Vinnie my mind's made up. I owe him that much. I mean, he ain't so stupid he don't know something's going on, but it ain't right not to tell him straight out.

And I can't wait much longer, 'cause I'm already wearing my clothes with safety pins at the waist to keep 'em closed I'm getting so fat. I'm afraid people'll start noticing, although right now they been so busy making cracks about my haircut they haven't said nothing yet. So I'm deciding as I'm leaving work that I gotta go right home and call Vinnie, and I almost jump out of my skin when I see him sitting in the lobby waiting for me.

It's just so strange seeing him here, he's never been to the office. People are bumping into me getting off the elevator 'cause I can't move for a second. I'm just staring at him and what I'm thinking is, he looks good. I mean, I'd be happy to see him if I wasn't about to fucking break his heart. He's walking over to me, wearing a beige shirt and black slacks and he looks nice. A hell of a lot better than any of the guys they got around here.

"You gonna say hello or what, Tina?"

"Whaddaya doing here, Vin?"

He shakes his head. "Whaddaya think?" We stand there like dopes for a second, then he leads me outside.

"Hey, I'm sorry," I tell him as we walk away from the building. "I know I been hard to pin down lately, but it's like I said. I just needed some time by myself."

"Bull*shit*."

"Why is that bullshit?" I sound all huffy, but I don't mean it. Of course it's bullshit. You love somebody, you wanna be with them. It don't take a genius to figure that out.

"Look, you wanna go for a drink or something?" I'm trying to be nice.

"No, I ain't got time for that. I had to leave a job early, a big renovation in Park Slope. People got a perfectly nice house but they wanna put in everything new—two bathrooms and a kitchen. I must of stood for an hour waiting for you."

"Jesus, Vin, I didn't know you was coming."

"Yeah, well, let's just get going." He starts heading west. "I just hope to God they haven't fucking towed the van."

"Christ, Vin! You drove into midtown rush hour?"

"Yeah. I ain't going down in no subway and rub shoulders with a bunch of animals. And you don't gotta neither once we're married."

I don't say nothing. I got enough to do just to keep my feet moving one in front of the other. We go all the way over to Madison and then start walking uptown. Vinnie digs in his pocket and hands me a piece of paper.

"Here. I figure I better take care of everything now, you been acting so weird. Here's a list of people I gotta invite to the wedding. My sister helped me. She wants to know also if she's gotta wear some special color or something or if it's all right to wear anything."

"Oh, Vinnie." He's got me crying now.

He puts his arm around me. "Tina. Sweetheart. You gotta pull yourself together. I know you got a lot on your mind, but you gotta take care of things."

I just nod my head and we keep walking. He's parked all the way the hell up at a construction site on Fifty-third. But I have to hand it to Vinnie. The van's still there, safe and sound. He's pretty smart. Not even the police gonna mess with a plumber.

We get in and it takes Vinnie a while to pull out into traffic. Then we get stuck on Fifth for what seems forever.

"So you gonna talk to me, Tina?"

"Yeah, sure, Vin."

"Hey, are you okay?" He touches my shoulder real gentle. A sweetie, this one. I feel like I'm out of my mind to be doing this.

"I'm fine, Vin. It's just that I been thinking about this, Vin, and shit, I don't think it's a good idea our getting married, you know? I don't think we'd be good for each other." I can hardly get the words out.

He just grips the steering wheel hard and don't look at me.

"I don't believe this," he says finally. "I don't fucking believe this."

"Please, Vin."

He's shaking his head, keeping his eyes straight out on the cars in front of him.

"Do you know what it is to love somebody, Tina? Huh, do you? 'Cause I don't think so. I don't think you ever loved me one fucking minute of your life, 'cause if you did, you couldn't be doing this to me now."

I'm hysterical, and maybe it's good I can't say nothing, just let him get it off his chest. The two of us in his blue van filled with augers and faucets and elbow sockets and blowtorches and tube cutters and wrenches and O-rings and all that shit in the middle of a traffic jam on Fifth Avenue. I'm looking out the window and there's Saks and there's Rockefeller Center with that statue of what's-his-name, the one carrying the world on his back. And I'm thinking, that must be a bitch in this heat. I mean, at a time like this, you never know what stupid thing is gonna pop into your head.

"Tina! Listen to me! You gotta think this over some more."

"I thought it over plenty, Vin. You gotta try to understand."

"I don't understand shit. What are people gonna say? They're gonna think there's something wrong with me, or I'm like this horrible creep or something you won't marry me and you're knocked up. Tina, don't be stupid, don't be crazy!"

"It don't matter what people think, Vin."

He just lets out a sigh and hits the steering wheel hard with the heel of his hand.

"Vinnie, you're a great guy. You're gonna find somebody better in about two minutes."

"Like you found somebody?"

"What?"

"You heard me. This has gotta be about another guy. What a jerk I am! Maybe it ain't even my kid!"

"Oh, Vinnie, please, it ain't like that, not really."

I can tell he's crying, but I can't look at him.

"You know," he says real soft, "I don't even think that.

But it would be better. I could even understand it a little. But that you just don't wanna marry *me* . . ."

And that's all we say. We're silent the whole ways home. Vinnie keeps checking his watch all the time, like he can't believe how long it's taking. I don't need to check what time it is. I fucking know. It's the fucking end of the world.

Chapter 24

When I get home I just about got the strength to open up a box of crackers. I sit in the kitchen eating Triscuits like some kind of machine, not thinking about nothing. But then Jeannie calls and I can't stop myself, I tell her I just broke up with Vinnie.

"You did what?"

"Please, Jean, I'm real sad right now."

"*You're* sad? You ever stop to think what other people feel?"

"Jean, don't lecture me."

"Fine, you go ahead on your own like always. But just one thing, Tina. You gonna tell Pop? You gonna stand there and tell him after all he did for you he's gonna have to be ashamed in front of the guys he works with? Who the fuck are you to do something like that?"

"Who am I?" I says. "I'm fucking scum, okay? You happy now? What do you want from me, Jeanette? I don't love Vinnie. Even with his kid inside of me I don't love him. I can't marry him with my eyes wide open. Pop'll get over it, okay? Just don't aks me to give up my whole fucking life."

Don't she know I don't wanna hurt Pop after all he went

through with Ma? I mean, if it wasn't for him, me and Jeannie never would of had a chance. Maybe I don't think I'm doing nothing wrong, but I know it ain't gonna look that way to him.

Even so, I can't believe how pissed she is at me. She don't even care if Donna and Joey hear everything.

"You know what Nick's gonna do?" she aks.

"I don't give a shit what Nick does."

"Yeah? Well let me tell you. He's gonna laugh his fucking head off."

"Thanks a lot, Jeannie." She's really busting my chops. But I get her to promise she won't tell Pop nothing, and believe me, she's tempted. I guess we been fighting about one thing or another since the day I was born. But me and Jeannie always had a good time together.

Now I can't settle down. I have this real tense feeling like I gotta do something but I don't know what, and all's I can think of is to call Grandma up and let her know the wedding's off. It's stupid, I know, but this way I'll get it over with.

First thing she says straight off is, "He walked out, huh? He wanted fresh goods."

"Thanks, Grandma. Jesus, did it ever occur to you that *I* walked out on *him*?"

"If that's the way you want it. So what are you going to do? I can't take you in, God knows. I've got enough on my hands with your mother."

"Why would I need you to take me in?"

"Because of the baby. You're pregnant, aren't you?"

She's too much. "How did you know?" I aks.

"Ha!" She calls out to Ma. "Joanie, Joanie," she yells, "you were right!"

I can't believe her, she sounds so happy.

"Everyone says you're mother's not right in the head, but she knows what she knows."

Talking to Grandma makes me sad as shit. It makes me wonder maybe I am crazy like Ma, like Pop's always worried about, because of what I done.

Chapter 25

I'm still afraid to tell Pop. So I go to Kathy. She knows something's up the second she opens the door, 'cause I never been to see her alone. Not in the two years she and Pop been married. She keeps offering me stuff to eat, but I'm too upset, so I just aks for some seltzer.

"Oh, Tina, I'm sorry," she says like it's a big deal. "We don't keep no seltzer. You want water?" I take the glass and tell her to sit down, but it's like telling a puppy, 'cause she's up again and pacing around the kitchen before I take a sip. When I tell her about not marrying Vinnie, and how I need her to talk to Pop about it, she lets out this funny laugh like she's strangling or something. "Are you sure, Tina?" But she can tell I'm sure.

She don't say nothing for a while, just leans back against the sink, her arms crossed in front of her. Finally, she shakes her head. "A baby on your own, Tina. Wow. I don't know. I don't believe it's sinful or nothing, but you gotta be ready for what people are gonna say."

I laugh. "They're already saying it. That I'm a jerk, crazy, selfish."

"And what about that you're a whore?"

"Kathy!"

"Not me, Tina. What, you're the first girl got pregnant without being married? But people like to feel superior. In a neighborhood like this"—she moves her eyes around the room—"whew!"

"This neighborhood ain't the whole world."

"No, but you live here, or just about live here. Where you are it's no better. Those old Italian ladies in black with the Blessed Virgin in their front yards, you think they're gonna smile at you, wanna know how you're doing? You think the men are gonna help you with your groceries, be respectful like you're some special deal? No, Tina. It'll be *puttana, puttana* behind your back."

I tell her, "I can handle it," but I feel like I'm choking on my words.

"And at work? You want the guys making remarks, the other girls treating you like you're some kind of disgrace? What about your boss? What's he gonna say?"

"You don't understand," I says to her. "I can go to work like always. They can't fire me for having a baby. These people don't care about that."

"People always care about that."

"Forget about it, Kathy," I says, real mad. "I don't know why I came. I'll tell Pop. I shouldn't never of aksed you."

"Come on, Tina. You know what I'm saying is the truth. I don't know, maybe things *are* different now. But, anyways, I'm not saying that you're wrong. I think you're right. You're a different type. You gotta do what's best for you. Your father married me when Vicky and everybody was telling him not to. *You* didn't want him to."

I start to argue, but she cuts me off.

"It's okay. The point is he did what he wanted. And we made it good, too, even though we can't have no kids. You got the strength to do what you want, nobody should tell you different."

I wanna aks her about the no kids part, but I don't wanna be here when Pop gets home. There's never enough time to get to everything. I mean, you see things, people, as you walk along, going about your business, and you wanna know, what's their story? Or let me stop and look at this. But you don't. You're always on your way somewhere or late for something or some shit like that. Anyways, I feel like chickenshit for leaving, but I figure, it'll be easier on everybody if Kathy breaks it to him.

Chapter 26

*E*ver see some of the stuff they try to get pregnant women to wear? Like those cheap, ugly blouses with checks and little collars, like you're so busy thinking about having a baby you forgot what clothes were or something? Like you got stupid? But the clothes Noah bought me, they're so beautiful I'd stay pregnant forever just to keep wearing 'em.

The guy just went out and got me a whole fucking wardrobe. Had it delivered by some messenger like in one of them old-time movies where all the women do is go shopping and then head home and wait for their packages to show up. He went crazy—he bought skirts and tops and dresses and pants and a coat and fucking fat-lady panty hose. I mean, I never had such nice clothes. Some of 'em came from Madison Avenue.

Like today, I'm wearing this gorgeous dark-blue plaid dress with these flowers embroidered on the top. I mean, I'm over four months now. My face don't look too much like a balloon. I figured everybody knew anyways, but when I walked in in this maternity outfit I thought their eyebrows would hit the fucking ceiling. I marched right into Dave's office to tell him, and he blushes and can't even look at me and I guess it was okay by him 'cause he didn't say nothing.

Then Frieda, the bitch, comes over and don't say great or congratulations or when are you due or any of that shit that people always say to pregnant women. No. She says, "Whatever happened to that nice boy you were going out with?" I mean, what can you answer? And don't aks me how the hell she knows about Vinnie. I can't remember telling her nothing about him. But that's Frieda all over.

The rest of 'em are trying to be cool and not say something stupid. So I guess it's not so bad. But I know that the guys are probably making dirty jokes in the bathroom. I mean, Tony'll stick up for me, but you can't change human nature.

I'm gonna go shopping at lunchtime just to take my mind off things. Find more stuff for the house. The books call it the "nesting instinct." Jesus. Where do they get it from? Do I look like a fucking bird? But I tell you, these last couple weeks, I can't stop buying. Not just things for the nursery—little baby night-lights and mobiles. No, I mean everything. I never really fixed up before. But I got the bug, all right. I took down those crummy posters, too. What a jerk.

It's good to be busy. I figure shopping's almost the same as a vacation. I didn't wanna go nowhere what with the new job and being pregnant and all. I'd rather spend my money on furniture. I went to one of them discount places and ordered a whole fucking houseful. Right out of the catalogs. Who knew there were so many different kinds of chairs? I must of spent five hours just picking out fabrics. I just kept turning the swatches over, looking at 'em again and again. Yellows, blues, pinks, greens. I love the way they feel. Fake velvet, polished cotton. Smooth, shiny, nubby. Sometimes you just gotta have something beautiful.

Meanwhile, I aksed Vicky to make me one of them wool throws for the couch, but I'm picking out the colors. Of course, first I had to calm her down 'cause she was pretty hysterical after Kathy told her about me not marrying Vinnie. I mean, just 'cause she never had the chance, she figures I'd grab at it. But she came around. Plus she loves to crochet.

Pop, though, he ain't forgiving me. I mean, I ain't welcome there, and Kathy can't fix it, neither. She's real broke up, too, because now she likes me. He throws me out and she's my friend. So she calls me up on the sly. She says he'll get over it. Great. Terrific. What I wanna know is, when.

It's funny. Here's a time I always thought brings people together, you know, everybody looking forward to a baby, and I'm out there hanging. My own father ain't talking to me. I mean, he never talked much to begin with. It was like you had to read between the lines, as they say. I always figured we was close, but with me and Pop, there was mostly white space.

Chapter 27

I'm going nuts with this feeling like I just gotta talk to Noah, tell him what's going on inside my head. Sometimes you just gotta speak to that one special person, like your words wouldn't have the same meaning if someone else heard them. I let some time go by, and then I start thinking that I don't give a shit if he thinks I'm a pain or what, 'cause if someone loves you, it should be okay to act stupid with them.

I wait till the end of the day and dial his number. This time Miss Shit-Don't-Smell puts me through.

"Tina! How are you feeling?"

"Okay, I guess. I mean, I didn't throw up or eat anything too weird this week."

"Great, great. It's great to hear from you."

"Yeah? If it's so great how come you never call me no more?"

"Tina, you know I've been busy. But I really want to know what's going on with you."

"Well, I'm pregnant, Noah. I figure that'll take up about nine months, give or take a day."

"Look, I'm due across town in about three minutes. Could we talk later?"

"When later?"

"Uh, in an hour? After work? At the Horse's Head."

"Yeah? You'll show?"

"Tina! Of course I'll show. You know me better than that."

And I hang up kind of happy that I'm gonna see him, but with this cold feeling in the middle of that, because no, no I don't know him.

I kind of stall around straightening up my desk, then go downstairs and stand in front of the building watching the people walk by, their jackets over their arms. It's gorgeous outside. The fall is the best time of the year. The air is still warm, but there's a change—it's not the same air's been here all summer.

Tony comes up behind me and taps me on the shoulder.

"Hey, go home already."

"I was just on my way."

"Walk you to the train?"

"Sure."

I can tell he's down. He don't like to admit it, but taking Lynn's crap gets to him. I mean, Tony'll get an idea for a story and assign it to one of the guys, or decide where something should run, or kill some article about friggin' printed circuit boards, and Lynn'll go behind his back and tell everybody to do the opposite of what Tony just said. And this is after Tony thought he'd cleared it. That stupid bastard Lynn makes everyone nuts, but Tony won't say boo about it. I don't get it. I mean, women always seem to need someone telling 'em what to do, making 'em feel bad. Maybe some guys do, too.

So Tony just talks on and on about some story idea about connectors, for godsake, like I could care. But sometimes it helps just to be with someone, I guess. I don't say nothing much neither, and he gives me a funny look when I get off the train in the Village, but I don't explain.

I sit at the bar and order a ginger ale and they serve it with this green plastic dolphin or something sticking out of it, which I like. Noah ain't here yet, so I'm listening to what other people got to say sitting around me. These two women—great makeup—are talking French or something on one side. Then on the other there's this guy and girl, the girl is really into what she's saying about some movie or some shit like that, only she keeps checking herself out in the mirror, seeing how her hair, which is blond and cut real short except in front, falls across her face. And she's saying something like, "Yeah, when they showed that little baby like looking at his hands and talking, man, it torpedoed my reality."

And I'm thinking this is the kind of thing makes people put up with all the crap about New York, and I'm feeling pretty good, and then I see Noah walk in and my heart just starts dancing. I mean, you try to be cool.

He comes over and hugs me and kisses me and for a second I feel better. And he looks me over and it makes him happy just to see me. That's real. But I'm thinking, with Noah it's like a kid sitting in a classroom and when the teacher calls his name he pays attention, but after a little while he turns away and starts daydreaming out the window.

We go sit down and he's telling me some story about some mixup at the hotel in L.A. last time he was there and I can't be bothered I'm so nervous.

"Noah?"

"What, Tina?"

"You notice I didn't get married?"

"Oh. Of course. I mean, that's great. It's the best thing. I always knew it. And you must have felt that all along, right?"

"Jesus Christ, Noah! That all you got to say about it?"

"Tina, what's wrong? I'm so thrilled to see you. You look beautiful. I've seen women look like hell when they're pregnant, but not you."

I guess that should make me feel good, but it don't. I take the dolphin out of my drink and keep busy trying to make it stand on the table.

"Hey," Noah says touching my hand. "Don't be sad, little darling."

I look up at him and I feel like I'm seeing him across

the goddamn Grand Canyon except he's right next to me.
Like I'm still in the way things were, and he's in this other
place. It's like he's aksing for something, like he's giving
me this tiny opening, this one chance to say the exact right
thing and bring him back. Someone puts "True Colors"
on the jukebox and I almost laugh and I say, "I love you,"
under the music and I'm not sure he understands.

He's staring at me and he's about to answer, but some
guy he knows comes over. Jesus, can you believe it? Guy
named Howard something. Asshole or something like that.
And Noah don't get rid of him. He's talking to the guy.
Before I can figure what's happening, Noah's getting up
and kissing me and saying he'll call, he's gotta work with
this guy on some case right now, and this Howard's looking
at me like he'd be interested except he can see something
strange is going on, and they're gone.

I sit there like a dope sipping the warm soda, like someone who can't leave the scene of an accident after all the
bodies and rubble and crap have been cleared away. I can't
make myself believe Noah just left me like that.

I take myself home and call Fern pretty hysterical.

"Why?" I aks her, like she'd have the answer.

"I don't know, Tina. But some guys, they just play at
relationships. They try them on, see if they can get a perfect
fit. They see a button's loose, forget it. They can't be
bothered."

"But why did he start with me if he knew he wasn't
gonna stick around?"

"Don't you see? He thought he was. He liked the idea.
He liked the idea of himself being with you."

"Like he liked the idea of himself being with Adeena."

"Yup. You got it. She was your bright red flashing warning signal. You didn't look."

Suddenly all I wanna do is go to bed.

"I'm tired, Fern. I can't talk about this no more." And
I'm thinking, somebody's gotta come up with an easier way
to be a human being.

Chapter 28

You don't get no privacy when you're pregnant. Every so often Gene or somebody will come up and pat my tummy like it's public property or something. What is it with some guys? Like it's magic or something. Like I'm a goddamn rabbit's foot.

And total strangers think it's a reason to start a conversation. When are you due? Is this your first? You want a boy or a girl, but it don't matter as long as it's healthy. Jesus. And then the looks I get in the neighborhood, the tongues clicking, like it's their business. But I don't give a shit. I don't need them or anybody.

Although I'm glad Ange is back. It's not nice, really, 'cause it ain't so much for her company. She don't wanna talk much and Christ, you should see her. She was out for two weeks and it looks like she lost ten pounds. And her face don't look too good, neither. But she says nothing's wrong. I mean, Fern wanted to go to the police, but I told her forget about it.

So what I mean is, I ain't the office freak no more. Ange's more interesting.

But she don't feel like going out to lunch anymore,

Tony's busy with all this shit Lynn gave him to do, so mostly I go with Fern and Yoshi. Only trouble is, I feel like the fucking chaperon. But when I'm alone with him, he comes on to me. Nothing big, but like he can't help it. Fern's crazy about him, but I think he may be a bit of a jerk. I don't know. Maybe he's just trying to make me feel better. Like I'm sexy even though I'm pregnant.

Whatever it is. Today Fern's at a news conference so me and Yoshi are at Dim Sum. It's funny how the Italians and Chinese got the same taste. I mean, this place, with that fuzzy red wallpaper in fancy designs—flocked, they call it—and fake paneling around the walls, looks like it was decorated by my aunt Vicky. Except for the pictures of those old Chinese guys climbing up some hill.

Soon's we walk in, Yoshi starts flirting with the waitress. You never saw someone bring soup so fast. I tell you, Fern's got her hands full trying to catch this one.

"So, Tina," he says all sweet, spooning up the wontons. "Can I ask you just one question? What made you decide to have a baby?"

I almost spit out the mouthful I just took. I look at him like he's crazy.

"What? You think I planned this?"

He looks all innocent. "I don't know. A lot of single women are having kids. I mean, you're smart. You must've been on birth control, right? I mean, I guess I'm being nosy, right? I should mind my own business?"

He's got a smile like a little boy you can't be mad at when he's naughty 'cause he's just so damn cute.

I don't say nothing. To tell the truth, I'm thinking maybe I *did* decide without even knowing it. You know how it is when someone says something like that. Like maybe they know you better than you know yourself. But then he leans closer and says, "Unless maybe you thought the guy was going to marry you because of the baby. Jesus, Tina, you're a beautiful woman, you didn't have to resort to that."

I never felt like killing nobody before, but I feel like it

now. "You bastard! What the hell gave you that idea? Who the hell are you to talk to me that way?" I don't care who hears.

"Easy, girl. I was just suggesting a possibility. Come on, Tina, it never occurred to you people were gonna think that?"

"I don't give a fuck what people think."

Of course I say this just as the waitress brings the rest of the food. She gives me a look.

"Who thinks that, Yoshi? You?"

"Naw. I heard a couple of the guys talking about it."

"What couple guys?"

"Never mind."

"You fucking reporter. You think I been here three years and don't know what you're doing? What, the guys take a bet you could get the story outta me? Is this a fucking search and destroy?"

He gives me that cutesy-pie smile again. I'm ready to smash his face.

"The pricks." Jesus, to think people had the wrong idea. I wanna cry. That's fucking being a woman. You can't never do nothing 'cause you always wind up fucking crying.

"Tina, come on. You work with somebody, you're curious."

"You're full of shit."

"Okay, Teen. Don't be mad. I just wanted to hear your side. I know you could marry anyone you wanted. Fern told me about how the guy wanted to marry you."

"So what the fuck was all this about? You just wanted to get a rise outta me? What kind of stupid stunt is this? You think I got no feelings? Jesus, Yoshi, I thought you was a friend or something."

He looks down. "I'm sorry," he says real low. "I thought Fern was just defending you, trying to make you look good in an awkward situation. I just wanted the real story, to hear it from you."

Well, maybe he's sorry, but I can't stop being mad.

"You wanna know why I'm having this baby? Okay, I'll

tell you." He don't say nothing and I let him have it. "So I could get away from bastards like you!"

I mean, I guess I should get up and leave or something, but the food's already here and I'm starved and besides that would waste my whole lousy lunch hour. He's just looking at his egg roll like he's dying to take a bite out of it but isn't sure it would be too cool to do it. He's just a guy. And really, I'm not even that mad at him. It's like that time with Vinnie at the Mt. Etna. I don't care no more what Yoshi thinks about me. Like all the feeling left me. Left me cold. I look at Yoshi. I mean, what does it matter? He's Fern's problem.

Chapter 29

It's funny, when something happens to you, it's like that's all you can see. When Ma went away the first time, I remember seeing all these mothers and daughters all over the place—going shopping, walking arm in arm. Or all the time I'd think I'd see her on the street and she was like a normal person, and just about to go to the movies or take the bus or something.

Now the world is full of pregnant ladies waddling around with their hands pressed against their backs. All these big bellies bobbing up and down Third Avenue. Or you're standing on the train real mad 'cause no one gave you a seat, and there's three other girls in the car more pregnant than you. I mean, a lot of times people do give you seats. Teenage boys, girls. Spanish guys, sometimes black guys. White women. White men, forget about it.

I'm taking the subway back from Dr. Bliss. There's an ad for Planned Parenthood in Spanish across from me. I think it's saying something like if you think you're pregnant come see us. But what I'm noticing is that in Spanish, pregnant is *embarazada*. Embarrassed. Why? Why should someone be embarrassed? Because you had sex? Because people know you're not married? I could care. I can live without fucking Mrs. Gentile saying "Good morning" to me.

Maybe that shit should bother me more. But I'm too happy today. There's something alive inside me. My baby. Me and my baby. *My baby does the Hanky Panky. Yes sir, that's my baby now. You must have been a beautiful baby.* I heard its goddamn heartbeat in the examining room. Real fast, like it's growing so quick nothing'll stop it. Strong. Maybe a boy, then.

I already gained twenty pounds. Dr. Bliss says I better slow down. I got almost four more months. I feel pretty good. I feel excited. I mean, people on the street, they see you, and they know: There's a person something big's gonna happen to them. I can feel the baby move, too. I told Jeanette. I wanted her to know even if she's been a real pill. I called her right up at eleven o'clock at night the first time I felt it. Like a little fish swimming in the sea.

It made me feel bad about Vinnie. I mean, he would of loved that. But I heard he's seeing someone else who won't let him near me. Little bitch. Well, what the hell did I expect?

Ange has started aksing me about names. The baby's the only thing seems to cheer her up. She's sure it's a boy. She does this thing where she sniffs your hair and swears she's always right. So maybe I should name it after Pop, except I hate the name Salvatore. Ange says maybe a saint's name, but I don't know about that. I want something classy.

Today me and Ange are working late. They dreamed up a special issue on some fascinating topic like computer-integrated manufacturing to try and get more ads, and we're running around like crazy. But I'm glad to be busy, and I'll bet she is, too. I mean, any excuse to keep away from that bum she lives with.

Anyways, we're on our way out and we get all the way to the lobby and everything and, sure enough, it's raining. I mean, maybe if we had a window you could see something out of I might of known. Ange is carrying her umbrella, but not me, so I turn right around and go back up to get it, but Ange is in a hurry all of a sudden and don't wanna wait. Like any excuse not to talk to me alone. Although, shit, it is almost seven-thirty. I tease her has she got a date or something, but she gives me a funny look so I back off. Jesus, she sure is touchy sometimes.

So I'm dragging myself off the elevator and I'm hearing voices and don't aks me why, but I stop just before the last turn into the office right by Gene's desk. And believe me, he hates sitting right there where everybody has to pass him all the time. Except when he's not busy. Then he stops anyone who walks by so's he can talk your ear off. Never occurs to him maybe *you* got something to do.

I'm standing there and I'm seeing Frieda all the way off in the far corner crying at her desk. And that's not even the whole of it. Lynn's standing over her like patting her shoulder, smoothing her hair. And it sounds like he's saying, "It's okay, Freddy. Don't cry, Freddy." Lynn and Frieda, for Chrissake.

It's like time has stopped. I can't quit looking at them, but then I feel all warm, hot, like I can't breathe and I gotta get out into the air. I'm backing away praying they can't hear me. So I'm stuck by the goddamn elevators without my fucking umbrella and sweating like a pig in my coat. My big, beautiful, black coat that Noah got me, the fucker.

I go back down. I don't give a shit if it's raining. I'm thinking about poor Frieda. Jesus, she's been here, what? Fifteen years? Fifteen years working with Lynn and loving him for Chrissake all that time? Lynn? In love with Lynn? And seeing him marry somebody else and have kids? Jesus, he can't be sleeping with her, can he, the bastard? I tell you, it'd take a lifetime to figure it all out.

Chapter 30

When I hit the lobby I'm thinking maybe I better wait it out or try to find one of those guys sells three-dollar umbrellas on the corner when I see Ange coming back in. She's looking at me kind of ashamed. "Sorry, Tina," she says. "I shouldn't of left you like that, pregnant and all in the rain."

"It's okay, Ange. I know you can't hang around too late."

"Naw. It ain't that." She shakes her head and I can see she's gonna cry.

"Jesus, Ange, what's going on with you? You come back to work after two weeks like nothing's happened, but you looked like shit and you wasn't fooling no one. Can't you even tell *me*? We used to be buddies, you know? I mean, if you can't tell me, who can you tell, right?"

She just keeps shaking her head and I don't know whether she's agreeing or what. She looks up to see who's around. Only Clinton, the night guy, just waiting to give shit to anybody tries to enter the building without signing in. Christ.

"He moved out," she finally says.

"What? Who?"

"Jimmy. He left me."

"*He* left *you*? Jesus, that's the most fucked-up thing I ever heard. Why, Ange?"

Now she's really crying. Shit. I turned on the tap or something. I pull her over away from that nosy Clinton who's got nothing better to do than stare at us.

"He left me . . ." she sobs. "He left me for this, this woman."

I don't have nothing to say, but I hate the guy. I mean, I wanna drive a knife through his heart right then and there. That's the only thing would make me feel better.

"That lousy bastard."

"I tried, Tina. I tried for so long to give him what he wanted. I just wasn't pretty enough or something. He says I was never good, you know, never good at, at, you know, sex and stuff. He says no one'll have me now. Oh, Tina, you can't tell nobody." She grabs my arm.

All I can do is hold her. "Ange, it's okay," I tell her. "You'll be fine. You don't need him, really, Ange. Get rid of him. Get a divorce."

She pulls away. "Oh, Tina, you know I can't do that. I'm a Catholic, remember?"

What can I say? Like no Catholic never got no divorce before. It's like she can't let go, you know what I mean?

"Ange, please, you're better off without him. Why should you feel so bad about yourself? Who needs that?"

"I feel bad I didn't make it work. I mean, I know Jim's not perfect, but he's provided for me and the kids for a long time. He can be real nice, Tina. You don't know the whole story. Just 'cause *you* don't care what people think don't mean it's right for the rest of us. Just don't say nothing, okay? I know he'll get tired of her pretty soon. Then he'll come back. I know he loves me. I'm the only one for him."

She's making herself feel better. It's too much for me. It's like a wall going up between us. It's almost like trying to talk to Ma. How can someone look normal, work, raise kids, and be so crazy? It don't make sense.

Ange looks at me funny. "I thought you went upstairs for an umbrella."

I smile and shake my head. "Wait till you hear this. You won't believe it."

And then I'm telling her about Lynn and Frieda and we walk out together under Ange's umbrella, laughing, and we're safe for now.

Chapter 31

I sit at home in front of the TV eating olives and thumbing through this fashion-school catalog I picked up at lunchtime last week. I mean, what the hell, right? But I must of drifted off right there on the couch 'cause the next thing I know I hear the phone ringing. It's Pop. Even half-awake I figure something's up because he hasn't exactly been talking to me.

"What is it, Pop? You all right? Kathy?"

"Yeah, we're fine. But your grandmother, Tina. She's dead."

I'm real sad. I mean, Grandma was pretty awful, especially lately, but she was still my grandma.

"What about Ma?"

"They're looking for her."

"Whaddaya mean?"

"Look, Tina, just come down here. Maybe Vinnie could take you."

"Vinnie? Pop, what are you talking about?"

"Oh. I forgot. Just get here, Tina, okay?"

What can I say? I call the car service. When we get to Ma's house, there's a couple of police cars outside. All the neighbors are standing around like somebody planted them there. I see people looking out their windows. Jesus. Something bad happens, everybody wants a piece of the action.

Upstairs, Pop is sitting on the couch talking to a policewoman. Kathy's standing in the kitchen, her arms wrapped around herself. She hugs me when I come in.

"Thanks for getting here, Tina. Your father's real upset and this place gives me the creeps," she whispers. "It's so dirty." Then she makes a face like maybe she shouldn't have said nothing. Shit. Who cares about that now?

I aks Pop what happened.

"They don't know, yet. Maybe a heart attack. Today, yesterday, even. A neighbor saw the door was open and yelled to see if they was okay. She got no answer, so she went in. Found your grandmother on the kitchen floor. Joan, uh, your mother wasn't here."

I look hard at Pop. "Ma?" I'm trying to talk low. "Did Ma . . . ?"

"What, Tina?"

"I'm worried maybe she did something." I half look at the policewoman. Here's a cute little blonde in this ugly uniform. Who can figure it?

She answers me. "We're guessing Mrs. Scacciapensieri found her mother dead, panicked, and walked out."

I think all of us are a little shocked by hearing Ma called that. It's been a long time since anyone thought of her as "Mrs." anything.

The policewoman is still talking. "Apparently she's under medication . . . ?"

I guess that's tact. "Yeah," I says. "For being nuts."

Pop don't like that. "Tina!"

"Oh, come on, Pop." He don't say nothing. "By the way, Pop. How come they called you?"

"She had my name and number on the refrigerator."

"Yeah? I guess on account of the money."

He gives me an angry look and I see him glance over to Kathy.

She shakes her head. "I knew it, Sal. Don't worry about

it. I know you had to." She gives a little laugh. "It was just probably more than I thought."

Pop's gonna say something but then two policemen come in with Ma between them looking like something the cat dragged in. I mean, she's been out in the rain and is soaked. All I can think of is what she used to say when me and Jeanette was kids: "Don't you know enough to come in out of the rain?" She looks at us like she never seen any of us before.

I go over to her. "Ma?"

She laughs and tries to shake off the cops holding her. "Don't think you whores have got me now. I know what kind of place this is. I won't be their whore. I told them. I won't pull down my pants for nobody, fucking bastards. Fucking NAACP bastards. Fucking eleven ninety-nine union bastards. I know what they're doing. Right in front of City Hall, too. All of 'em together, the schvartzes and spinyuckas and yids and polacks and wops, the dirty wops, the whole stinking mess of 'em. Won't go to the hospital no more, fucking whorehouse. They're all over the place, just waiting to stick it into you.

"They come here sometimes and do it to Momma. She lets 'em do it to her, the old cunt. The old stinking, dirty cunt. Let them have her, the bitch. She wants it. She lets 'em come in. She lets 'em fuck her. With their big pricks. She likes their big pricks. She lets 'em do what they want. Oh, I hear it. Momma, I hear it. I hear you. I never let no one touch me in my life, you hear me? Never let them near me. I'll cut 'em. I'd bite it off. Ha. The whole bunch of 'em. The mayor, too. Big fat pricks, marching in the Macy's parade. But I'm hiding. I got my own balloon. Can't find me now, Momma. Can't bring me down now."

Chapter 32

So the cops take Ma away. Bellevue. Pop won't look at her. He won't look at nobody. Kathy's trying to figure out something to say. "I guess she's upset, huh?" For some reason, that cracks me up. I'm laughing, and every time I try not to, it's no good, I just crack up some more. Kathy smiles, but not Pop. I'm trying to say, "I'm sorry," when he gets up and slaps me. That makes me stop.

"You're just like her."

"Sal!" Kathy's so scared she can't move.

"Why must she always act crazy?"

"Sal, stop it!"

I can't say nothing, 'cause now I'm crying too hard. He never hit me before in his life. Then I know how much I hurt him, and how sorry I am. He just stands there looking at me and then *he* starts crying. "Oh my God, the baby. I'll kill myself if I did anything to the baby."

I put my arms around him. "It's okay, Pop, it's okay. You didn't hurt nothing," I tell him. I kind of hand him over to Kathy and figure I better change the subject. "Pop, where's Jeannie? How come Jeannie ain't here?"

He's wiping his nose. "It was too far for her to come. She's got two kids, Tina."

"That supposed to be a reason?"

"Don't start again, Tina." He's not so mad anymore, just worried I'm gonna make another scene.

"Okay, Pop."

I go to the kitchen to call Jean. I think about Grandma falling down on the old linoleum, lying there with the teakettle in her hand. Lying there in her yellow apron and orange housecoat. Jesus.

When Jeannie answers, I let her have it. "Whaddaya mean it was too far to come? Staten Island ain't the fucking end of the earth! I came from Brooklyn, for godsake!"

"Who said I said it was too far?"

"Pop. That's what Pop said."

"Well that's what *he* said. *I* said I wasn't coming."

"Fuck you, Jean. She was your grandmother, too!"

"Oh yeah? Well maybe I am sorry about Grandma, but I won't go near Ma. And don't you lecture me, Tina. You was too young to remember things. You didn't have no kids in school laughing at you 'cause she was walking around one day in her nightgown. Yeah, I never told you that."

"Christ, Jean," I say, "that was years ago." But it takes the heart right outta me.

"It's just that you should be here, Jeannie, with the family."

"Excuse me, Tina. My family's here. I'm looking at 'em."

"Oh would you stop with that crap already!"

"Yeah, to you it's crap. You got no idea what having a family means, Miss Independent."

I feel like I'm gonna bite her head off, so I shut up for a minute to cool off.

"Tina, you hear me?"

"Oh, Jeannie. You just can't walk away from this. That never solved nothing."

"Yeah? And what about running right smack into trouble with your eyes open? That better?"

How come every goddamn conversation with my family turns into a contest? I'm not trying to win nothing.

"Jean, I don't think Ma'll be at the funeral. I don't think she'll, uh, be feeling up to it. Will you please at least come?" I'm not angry no more.

She's calmed down. "Sure, Teen. I'm sorry Grandma's gone. But you know, the old lady was off her rocker, too."

"You're telling me."

I'm kind of hoping she'll say something more about it, about Ma and Grandma and what's happened. I mean, it's funny, something as big as Ma's being mental in our family, and we never really talk about it. It's like we don't know how to start. But she don't go into it. All she says is, "How's Pop?"

"Okay."

"You?"

"Okay, I guess."

"You didn't need this with the baby and all."

"I'm okay."

"This sort of thing is harder when you're alone."

"I said I was okay, Jean."

She lets it drop. "I guess this kills Thanksgiving, huh?"

I have to laugh. "Yeah."

"Call me about the funeral."

"Okay, sure."

"Ah, Teen."

"What, Jeannie?"

"I ain't mad no more. So don't be mad at me, okay?"

"When am I ever mad at you?"

"Come on, Tina."

"We're sisters, Jeannie. We can give each other shit and still not mean nothing by it."

Chapter 33

We gotta get a rabbi, which is weird. I aks Fern to give me a name. I'm using her doctor and now her rabbi. Let me just get the name of the guy who cuts her hair and get it over with.

Turns out, though, the rabbi's a woman. Fern says she's real nice. "Very supportive." Sounds like a goddamn Playtex bra. Cross My Heart. Anyways, she tells me what to do about the arrangements and when she shows up at the funeral home I don't know it's her because she looks maybe eighteen. Pop looks real put out I got this woman and Nick's making cracks about maybe the Jews aren't so bad after all if the rabbis are so good-looking. Jesus. I'm glad to see everyone's in the mood for a funeral.

It's real small 'cause Grandma didn't know nobody and Ma's her only kid. She had a boy died real young. Maybe that's what started the trouble.

Jeannie decided to bring Donna along for some reason. Nick was against it and for once I agree with him. But Donna's a real smart kid and you can't hide nothing from her. I'm happy to see her. She's all excited about the baby but she don't get it that I'm not married. She thought you had to be married to get a baby. Well, I used to, too.

She's real wide-eyed at the cemetery and aksing can the people get out of the ground and where do their souls go and will we all die and will Grandpa die next 'cause he's oldest and Joey the last 'cause he's youngest except for Aunt Tina's baby. And what will happen when all the people on the earth die?

She thinks the cemetery's a pretty neat place all around. Then she really gets a kick out of washing her hands at the curb before we go inside back at Pop's house. She thinks it's real funny washing up outside. *I wash my hands of it*—that's what it makes me think of. I think to aks the girl rabbi what it means, but don't bother.

Anyways, the cemetery's in Brooklyn, so we go back to Pop's place after, even though I offered. They still treat me like a kid, you know? Kathy's made some food and we're standing around with paper plates and cups in our hands and Jeannie comes over and pulls me aside.

"Teen, I been talking to Nick," she says, her voice real low.

"Yeah? So? You want a reward?"

"Funny. I been talking to him about the baby."

"Joey?"

"No, stupid. Your baby."

"Yeah? What about it?"

"He thinks maybe we could take it. Give it a home."

I don't know what to say I'm so angry. I just stare bug-eyed at her.

"Teen? Don't you think it's a good idea? I told you you was always wrong about Nick. I mean, I wasn't gonna have no more babies, but this is different."

"Jeannie, I can't believe you."

"Don't sound like you're mad, Tina. I thought you'd be grateful."

"Christ Almighty, Jean. *I'm* gonna give the baby a home. The baby's fucking mine! Has everybody in this family lost their minds?" I'm yelling now and Kathy comes over to see what's wrong.

"Jeannie," I'm saying, "don't never talk about this again, okay?"

"Talk about what?" Kathy wants to know.

"Forget about it," Jeannie says and she starts to cry. "It wasn't such a bad idea, Tina. You could of visited all the time. It's not like you never would of seen him. It's just that you're not really prepared. And Donna and Joey would play with him. We'd give him a family."

"I ain't no fucking surrogate mother, Jeannie," I scream at her. "Do I look like fucking Mary Beth Whitehead? Huh? Do I?"

Now Jeannie's crying like crazy and Kathy's standing there with her mouth hanging open. Finally, she looks at Jean and shakes her head. "We can't have Tina's baby, Jeannie. It's Tina's baby."

Donna comes over and hugs Jean around the waist. She starts singing something from some kid's tape or something.

> In this old world take my advice,
> You'd better be happy when the weather's nice.
> There'll be rain tomorrow no one can doubt,
> So be happy now when the sun is out.

Fucking right. It's my fucking baby.

Chapter 34

Pop wants to know where I'm gonna put my kid. I mean, I'm gonna put her in her crib. At home. I don't see what the problem is. I guess he thinks I should move to a bigger place, but this place is fine. I mean, it's only got the one bedroom, but the hall's so big I can put up a screen or something and put her crib there.

I mean, it's no big deal. You look at life like there are problems, believe me, you'll find them. Jeannie don't say nothing more about taking the baby. I think what with the funeral and all she didn't know what she was doing. But now she's going crazy buying a ton of baby stuff—stretchies and bottles and toy animals—and she's even getting me all the things that go with the crib, like a quilt and bumpers. And that's expensive. I can just imagine the fight she had with Nick over that. Pop says he won't give me nothing till the baby comes 'cause he's superstitious or some shit like that.

I go to bed early most nights, reading up on breast feeding—they got whole books about it, if you can believe it. I'm all settled in when the bell rings. Who the hell is it at this hour? I mean, maybe it's only ten o'clock, but on a fucking Wednesday? First I get scared, you know? Pregnant ladies gotta be careful.

Then I'm all excited that maybe it's Noah. You'd think I'd give up already. But, shit. It's Vinnie. He looks awful.

"Come on in," I says, trying to sound like I'm happy to see him. "How are you?" He's looking at me like he's gonna eat me.

"You look great, Tina."

"I'm fat as a house."

"Naw. I like it."

"Thanks, Vin."

"How are you?"

"I'm good, Vin."

"You look good."

He looks around like he don't know where to put himself. He's breaking my heart. But I feel like he's a little kid, you know? Not no husband or anything.

"What's up, Vinnie?"

"Nothing, Tina. Just wanted to see you. See how you're doing. How the baby's doing."

"We're good. Been taking good care of myself. I'm going to these Lamaze classes, you know? To get ready."

He shakes his head like he don't know but ain't really listening anyway. I guess I shouldn't talk about it.

"I been seeing someone else," he tells me.

"I know, Vin. You got a right."

"I know I got a right."

I'm thinking, I could of married this guy. We could of been married by now in some nice little house. The thing is, you get to feel like shit either way. I mean, if we was married, I'd feel like shit 'cause I didn't wanna marry him. And now I feel like shit 'cause he's so sad. Sometimes I wonder if it matters what you do.

He sits down on the couch and picks up the copy of *American Baby* I left lying around and looks at the pictures, his face kind of scrunching up. I mean, he looks like somebody died.

"Vin. It's good to see you. Really. I'm glad you ain't mad

no more. I'm sorry about what I done. I didn't wanna hurt you. But I never would of made you happy. You know that. I'm sorry about the baby. You'll have other babies. Maybe with that what's her name."

"Connie."

"Right. Connie."

"It don't feel right."

I sit next to him. What a honey. And that little bitch'll use him like a rag. "It'll be all right. It'll be like real life. You'll see."

He's sobbing. "Tina, couldn't we . . . ? Couldn't you . . . ?"

"Oh, Vinnie." We sit there for a while. He stops crying. He looks awful. Worse than when he came in.

"Okay, Tina. I get the message. I should never of come."

"I'm sorry, Vinnie."

"Sorry's not enough."

I can't help it, but I laugh. "That's what Donna always says."

Now he's pissed off. "You know what Connie says?"

Like I care. "No. Tell me what Connie says."

"She says it's not my kid. No way."

The fucking whore. But why get into it? "Is that what you came here to tell me?"

"Jesus, Tina, is it or isn't it?"

"You tell me."

"Stop your fucking games."

"Look, Vin, if it helps you to think the baby ain't yours . . ."

He don't answer for a while, just looks in my face like he could read the answer or something.

Then he turns away. "Tina, you ain't thinking about doing anything about it now, are you?"

"Doing anything about what? What are you talking about?"

"Like one of them paternity suits or something like that."

Jesus. She's a real prize. She's making sure.

"Tell Connie not to worry."

"Leave her outta this. This is between you and me, Tina."

"Yeah, sure, Vin. Just don't worry about it, okay?" I push myself off the couch. "And take care of yourself, Vin. You look terrible."

"No thanks to you."

I walk toward the door. "Look, Vin. I'm tired."

He don't get the hint. "You always gotta be different," he says to me, shaking his head. "Most girls get pregnant 'cause they want the guy to marry 'em. You get pregnant so's you can break up with the guy. It don't make no sense, Tina."

"Vin, we been over that already."

"I still don't get it."

He comes over to me like he's gonna grab me or something and I back away. I just want him to go so's I can be alone with my baby. "Me neither, Vin," I says as he walks out. "I don't get it neither."

I'm telling him the God's honest truth.

Chapter 35

It's a little strange going to the Lamaze classes with Fern. I mean, all the other girls, women, whatever, have their husbands or—excuse me—lovers, and I have her. It's just that it's so, what's the word? Intimate. Everybody sitting around talking about when the babies come out and breathing together and lying around in a circle on the floor. But what could I do? It's better than nothing. I mean, I guess I thought I'd go with Noah. I guess that was stupid.

And Fern was so hot to do it, I thought, why not? This is something I could do for her, if you see what I mean. Something she needed. So I never aksed Kath, although I thought of it. I would of liked Jeannie, too, but how the hell is she gonna come in from Staten Island and leave the kids? As if Nick would let her anyways. Any other time, I would of aksed Ange, but she's so gloomy lately. God, you'd think she'd be glad not to have that bastard around anymore.

I'm real excited. I been reading all this pregnancy stuff and following how Chicken Little is growing inside me, when the little fingernails are coming in. What's good is that by now everything's on, and so if something should happen—if the baby should be early—at least it would have a chance.

Only trouble is, people already started aksing me if I feel anything yet and has the baby dropped and when do I think it'll be—early or late or what? Jeannie calls every damn night. She's jealous about Fern and the classes, I can tell. Well. She could of offered.

I been real good about doing my exercises and shit and even went to visit the hospital like they tell you to. Big deal. Looks like a hospital. They got a birthing room that's supposed to be something special, but it looks like a room at the Howard Johnson's if you aks me. I'd rather have the baby in a real hospital room, delivery room, whatever.

I keep expecting Dr. Bliss to tell me something like he can tell how big the baby is or whether it's a girl or a boy or what day it's gonna come. But he says you can't know stuff like that. I can't believe what with science and everything it's all still such a mystery. I could of had an amnio, I guess, but Bliss said I didn't need one at my age. I mean, I thought I was old for having a kid but he says no. Everything's fine he says. Sure, everything's fine. I can hardly walk and feel like I gotta go to the bathroom every minute 'cause the Chick is pressing on my bladder. God. I saw a picture of what you look like inside with a seven-month baby. I mean, your lungs and stomach and everything are squished up, it's a miracle you can take a breath or eat a bite of something. I mean, I'm sorry I looked.

They're gonna give me eight weeks off from work. Big deal. But I'm lucky I'm getting that, 'cause before we got bought up some girls didn't get nothing. I mean, I don't even know if that's legal or what.

Frieda's like mad at me I'm gonna have this baby. Like I did it just to bother her or something. People are just too much. She gets on my nerves and I wanna open my mouth about what I saw with her and Lynn that night, really tell her off. I mean, what the hell right has she got to get on her hot horse if she's been having an affair with

Lynn all this time? It's funny, you know some people for
years, it's like you're always talking in some kind of secret
code. You never say what's really on your mind. But I can't.
I mean, I don't think she could take it. But the shit she's
been giving people, Jesus, am I tempted.

Fern's all in a huff 'cause she was supposed to get this
promotion before Christmas and it's pretty obvious Lynn'll
never give it to her. It's like I says to her, the fucking title
don't matter. I mean, does it matter you're an assistant
editor or an associate editor? But he made up these fucking
titles and other people have the fucking title so of course
she wants it. And forget about Dave helping her. That's
over long ago. I knew he wasn't a good bet. How the guy
ever decides which leg to put into his pants first in the
morning I'll never know.

She and Lynn had this big scene and she aksed why
wasn't she getting the promotion and he gave her some
bullshit that one of her stories was too short. Really. I ain't
kidding. That's what he said. So when she aksed how come
nobody told her to make it longer, he didn't have nothing
to say, and just said if she didn't like it she knew what she
could do about it. I tell you, the guy's a nut case.

But Fern's smart, and she backed down real fast so's
not to give the guy anything to fire her for. Thing is, he
won't let her go. But he won't give her anything good,
neither. That's his way. I mean, you'd have to practically
throw a fucking tuna fish sandwich across the room at the
guy to get fired, but you have to be free, white, male, and
twenty-one to get a decent beat.

Don't aks me why Tony stays. I tell him everybody's fed
up with Lynn, but he just shrugs, "He's not so bad."

"Oh come off it, Tony! He treats you like dirt."

"Back off, Tina. I know what I'm doing."

"Yeah? Then how come you stick around here? You like
being treated like garbage? That all you think of yourself? You're never gonna be able to do piss here 'cause he
won't let you. He's gotta be the goddamn king. Jesus, this
place."

He don't answer, but I can tell he's angry. Too bad. He needs shaking up.

Fern should just leave anyways, 'cause it looks like people are gonna be laid off, the industry's doing so bad. They're gonna have to cut the pages—the advertising's been going down and no one can sell space for shit, and maybe 'cause he's got nothing better to do Marv's been putting the moves on Angie, which she don't need right now. I mean, the guy's a total scuzz. He thinks he can get an easy lay 'cause he got word somehow her husband's out of the picture. Like she'd be so grateful someone paid some attention to her. Slipped her a quick one. What a sleaze. And the guy's married. The guy's got kids. Imagine what life in *that* family is like.

Jeanette says to take it easy and quit work. She says I'm crazy traveling in every day from Brooklyn. But what the hell am I supposed to do? Sit home and read *The First Twelve Months of Life* a million more times?

But it's true—I can't concentrate on nothing in the office, although Dave never seems to notice. I don't know what made him so afraid of his own shadow. I'm sitting here trying out names. Writing 'em out on my notepad. It ain't easy to come up with them, 'cause not too many things go with Scacciapensieri. Everybody says I should choose something real small and plain, but I say the hell with that. I been reading movie and TV credits and crap to look for good names. I'm kind of leaning toward Elizabeth. Or maybe Alexandra.

Fern says don't I need a boy's name, and I guess she's right. But I figure, if it's really a boy, I'll worry about it when it happens. She's real happy about the baby, I'll give her that. After work sometimes we go to eat and practice the breathing. Everybody thinks we're nuts. I'm feeling good she's gonna be there. I mean, I never even figured her for a friend. Maybe I should name the baby after her or something, but I don't know. Baby Fern? You see what I mean.

Kathy calls me up and reminds me to phone her right away if I feel anything and she'll come, too. So, I figure

I'm covered. She's been checking up on me. It's nice. It ain't Noah, but it's really nice. Now she aks about what I'm gonna do when I go back to work.

"What do you mean, Kath? I told you already. I'm gonna find some lady to watch the kid. Ain't that what everybody does?"

"I guess, Tina. But it's not cheap."

"Well, I guess not, but I'm hoping I'll find some neighborhood lady, middle-aged, wants something to do, likes kids, maybe wouldn't charge so much."

"Oh."

"Don't tell me I shouldn't leave the baby with a stranger, Kath. I don't believe in that shit. Besides, I can't afford not to go back. I figure maybe Pop's gonna have to lend me some money the way it is, I mean if you think he can."

"Maybe I could help you find someone."

"Sure, Kath, thanks. That'd be good."

"I mean if you think that's the best thing."

Now I'm getting annoyed 'cause I don't know what she's driving at.

"Shit, Kathy, it's a little late to be telling me I'm making some kind of mistake here. I thought it was pretty clear what I was gonna do."

"Don't get mad, Tina. That's not what I meant."

"Well, what did you mean?"

"I thought, maybe, I could help take care of the baby."

"Oh, Kath, sure. I mean, that would be so great, like if I ever went out or something again in my life. Thank you."

"Maybe during the day, too."

"But you're working."

"Oh, I don't care about that."

"Jesus, Kath, I never figured."

"Am I wrong to want to, Tina?"

Wrong? Shit! She's got me crying now.

"I can't talk now. Let me call you tonight, Kath. We'll work it out."

And I'm thinking, everybody's loving this baby already, and now I know I didn't do nothing wrong.

Chapter 36

I can't sleep hardly at all now. I can't get comfortable my belly's so big, and my mind is jumping around. I got this postcard from Noah. I mean, a lousy postcard. He's in Europe. Business or what, I don't know. Funny. I kept thinking I was gonna bump into him on the street or something, but the whole time he was away. I guess I should feel better he ain't here. Maybe he would of called if he'd been around. But I liked to think he was close by. Even if he don't give a shit no more. Nothing made me feel alone like getting that postcard.

Maybe Ma felt down like this, and that's how the craziness started. Just sitting and looking out the window at 3:00 A.M. with no light coming in. I wonder—did she try to tell anyone? I bet no one noticed, right off. Not in my family. They just left her out there alone in her nightmares.

Fern says, if you're schizophrenic, you're born that way, it's in your brain chemistry. Except it must take awhile to show. I guess that's why Pop was always so afraid, just waiting for me or Jeannie to wake up nuts one day.

I know I should feel bad for Ma. I do feel bad. It's just

that, mostly, I feel nothing. I'm not angry about it, the way Jeannie is. Except I think Pop got a raw deal.

Maybe I could of done something for her, but I don't know what. I think that's what got to Pop the most—always trying and nothing doing no good. I guess after a while he couldn't take it no more and got the divorce. I mean, it was his right, wasn't it? I'm glad at least that someone's taking care of her now. I wish they could give Ange some pills to get *her* head screwed on straight.

One day that dirtbag Jim's gonna kill her, that's the only thing's gonna put an end to it. And who am I to say anything, when I think about Noah, Noah all the damn time, think about everything he used to do to me? Touching me, shit, I can feel it. Here I am about to be a fucking mother, too. But even bringing myself off don't get me to sleep.

So I stay up and listen to the noises, imagining how cozy it'll be when the baby comes. Tell her, "Oh, that's the little dog next door. Don't let it scare you. That's a ship's horn. Yeah, you can really hear them sometimes." Sometimes I think I hear something. A break-in, you know? Then I get up and turn on the lights whoever it is should know there's someone awake in here.

Everybody says my place is too small, but I got a view worth a million dollars. I can see some of the Manhattan skyline from here. At this angle, all them buildings look bunched up together, ring upon ring, and even the World Trade Center don't look too bad, sticking up out of the middle. On rainy days, sometimes all you can see is the top of the towers rising out of the clouds. It's something.

At night, it's all lit up. The lights start to come on at dusk, and it's like the sunlight, fading, changes into little windows of electricity. Then the sky gets dark and the lights burn stronger.

But the early morning's even better. First everything's all gray, but then the towers start to shine pink in the dawn and then the other buildings shimmer like they're this giant mirage, about to float off into the air. So I sit by the window and watch.

Around seven o'clock, I call Jeanette. I know she's up because of the kids. Donna answers the phone.

"You have the baby, Aunt Tina?"

"Not yet, sweetie."

"Oh. I told all the kids about it at school. Can I bring in your baby for show-and-tell?"

"Well, we'll see, honey. What's that screaming?"

"Oh, it's only Joey. He banged his coconut."

When Jeannie gets on I aks her is the baby all right.

"Yeah, thank God. I tell you, Teen, you gotta watch 'em every second. You can't just hire some colored woman doing it for the money."

"Jesus, what's that colored woman shit? That don't sound like you. It sounds like Nick."

"Yeah, well, maybe just this once he's right, Miss Know-It-All."

"Come on, Jean. I don't wanna get into it. But let me tell you, I would love to have one of them women. I see 'em here sometimes, coming in and out of the brownstones. They do *some* job, talk to the kids real sweet with those beautiful voices they got. I couldn't even afford one of 'em."

"Yeah? So what are you gonna do? Jesus, Tina, the baby's gonna be here any second. You just don't plan nothing."

"I got someone."

"Yeah? Who?"

"Kathy."

"Kathy? Jesus Christ in heaven, Tina! She's a drunk!"

"Shut your mouth, Jeanette! I hope to God Donna didn't hear you say that."

"So what would it matter?"

"It matters 'cause it ain't true and I don't want her thinking nothing like that."

"Christ, Tina, sometimes you're just blind. You don't see what you don't wanna see."

"You're hardly the one to be accusing me, Jean."

"And what's that supposed to mean?"

"You know just what I mean."

"I face the facts, kid. You're off in some dream land."

"Right. Who's the one forgot she had a mother?"

"Don't talk to me about that."

"Oh, Jeannie, don't you see?"

"I don't see nothing. I see you thinking you can cause shame to everybody and do what you goddamn please and then think it's okay to have some drunk take care of your kid."

"Jean, she ain't had a drop since she and Pop got together."

"And just how do you know that, Tina?"

"I know. I can tell."

"You can tell shit."

"She'll be real good at it, Jeannie."

"Oh, Teen, she ain't even a relative."

Then she's gotta go on account of Joey crying again. Donna pushed him or something.

Now that I only got a couple more months at the office, I get ready for work pretty quick. I look forward to getting there, for godsake. Jesus, you never want something till you can't have it. Two months'll take me past my due date, just a little, but I wanted to make sure I didn't quit early and sit home twiddling my thumbs. This way I get all my time with the baby. You gotta figure it that way, what with the leave they give you being so short and all. I mean, it's like a fucking punishment.

I feel pretty bouncy, though, even without sleeping and even though I gained forty-five pounds. Yeah, I really did. But thin girls do that. I ain't apologizing.

I catch the subway and get to Grand Central early. It's crowded, but not so crazy like it gets around nine, so I'm walking slowly thinking about getting a doughnut or something when I see this woman dragging herself around and I swear I'm looking at Ma.

She's real skinny and sort of talking to herself. She don't look at nobody, but she's real involved in what she's saying. She ain't dressed too bad, with some kind of mustard-colored coat with a fake fur collar on, too big for her. Her hair's pitch black and she's got too much makeup on. She's carrying one of them promotional tote bags. It says MONEY.

Seeing her makes me go all cold and scared and I ain't gonna say nothing. I just wanna run in the other direction. But I force myself to go up to her and then I see it ain't really Ma. I'm so happy I aks this woman does she want anything. It's like she don't hear me at first, but then she says, "Gimme a candy bar."

So I take her over to this newsstand they got in the middle and I can tell people are staring at us. I mean, we're a prize pair. I got a belly sticking out halfway to Jersey and she's a friggin' nut case.

I get her the big Hershey's and I see they got a million magazines, so I buy a copy of the new *Parents*. I notice she don't smell too great and I aks how long she been here but she don't answer. She's just eating the chocolate and tearing off bits of the wrapper and dropping them on the floor. I bend down to pick it up and that ain't easy, let me tell you. She's making a real mess.

"Ma," I says, "just look at yourself. I'm ashamed of you."

I feel like a jerk for saying it, but she don't seem to notice. Nothing seems to bother her. I stuff a couple of dollars in her hand and leave her there. I feel bad, but I wipe my hand off real good on my coat. I'll wash when I get to the office.

Chapter 37

Ange is real down about Christmas, although to tell you the truth, I can't see why. I mean, the bum is out of the house, and she's gonna be with all her kids at Carla's. So what's bad? Plus, she's gonna be a grandma. Can you beat that? She's fucking forty-two years old.

She's seen the one with her husband. The whore. A real cheap type, you know what I mean. Bleach blonde and wears them real tight jeans with zippers at the ankles and high heels. And a short jacket even when it's snowing out in case maybe you can't see her butt. He didn't even bother leaving the damn neighborhood. He's gotta rub her face in it.

Ange don't even wanna go with us to the office party. I mean, it *is* pretty funny. They're having it at the Horn & Hardart. I'm not kidding. The fucking Automat. I practically fell on the floor laughing when they told us. I mean, they've pulled some pretty chintzy stunts here before, but this tops it. You should see who hangs out there. It's not exactly a festive atmosphere, if you know what I mean.

The parties are usually terrible, anyways. Everybody

stands around with nothing to say to each other, and the big boss goes to everyone to shake hands but don't know nobody's name and pretends like you're something really special and if the company had a good year, by Christ, he'd like to thank you personally for pulling it off. And then everybody feels real good and goose bumpy for about thirty seconds. But it's all bullshit, and they don't wanna know about it.

Fern is just dying for some time alone with Yoshi, or maybe for him to say something about going someplace after, but it's no go. I mean, the guy's been here a few months and there's girls from all over the company coming over to him. I hope Fern finally gets the picture. I mean, this guy goes through women like Kleenex.

Lynn's had a few by now and comes limping over like he's about to fall down, he's tipping so far to one side. He's all sweetness and palsy-walsy and aks how I'm doing like he cares more than anything in the world. He puts on a good show. But I can see it in his eyes. He thinks I'm dirt. He can't wait for me to leave. Too fucking bad.

"Tell me," he says, "are you going to take the baby to work with you like I read those black girls bring their babies to high school? That must be interesting, right?" He looks over to Gene and some of the other guys who are standing around like jerks and they all laugh.

"Yeah," Gene giggles, "the babies probably help them out on their algebra tests."

"That's it," Lynn says, turning to me. "Your baby could help you type. Maybe the baby would make decent coffee." No one laughs too much. I gotta give 'em some credit.

I give Lynn this sweet smile. "Gee, Lynn. That's a good idea. I'll bring the baby with me. I know that since you got all those kids and all, you must really like kids. I guess that's why you thought about it."

He's smiling like his stomach hurts and raises his glass. "Sure, sure. Let's all bring our kids in."

"Hey, I don't have any kids," Gene pipes in. "I mean, I'm not even married." Then he glances over to me and blushes, and everybody looks real uncomfortable and Lynn says something like, "Oh, oh," and Yoshi says, "Maybe you can rent a kid," and Fern says, "I don't think they'd let him." And Lynn laughs real loud at this because that's how he is. I mean, basically, he hates everybody.

I move away from them and go find Tony, who's standing by himself in a corner somewhere. Just like him, too. I mean, the guy's not exactly great at social situations. He's got a beer in his hand and I give him a look. His trouble is, they don't go to his head, they go to his belly.

And don't aks me why, but I start telling him this dream I had. I guess people do funny things at parties. But he's real interested so I'm telling him how I dreamed the baby was already born, and I heard it crying in another room—I guess I was in the old apartment where I grew up but not exactly like it, you know?—and so I tried to go to it, but it was like I was never getting any closer. And it was kind of dark and I kept getting more and more scared. I mean, I knew something was wrong, but I couldn't get to my baby. I couldn't find it. I couldn't help.

When I finish I feel kind of embarrassed like I told him something I shouldn't of, so personal and all, and I'm worried maybe it's a little crazy, too.

But he smiles and says, "I can understand having that kind of dream."

"Whaddaya mean?"

"I mean not feeling in control. Because with something like a baby, you really don't have much control, do you? I mean, I guess I never thought about it before, but even though you can be sure to eat certain things and check in with your doctor, things like that, you have no idea really of what's going on inside. This child growing inside you, sight unseen."

I smile back at him. "Yeah. It's weird, ain't it?"

"Are you very worried?"

"About what?"

"That something'll go wrong."

"Oh. I guess everybody thinks about that. No. Not too

worried. I don't know. I guess I'm just anxious to see her already. To hold her."

"Her?"

"Okay. It."

"Well, it's easy for me to say, but don't worry too much. I mean, I guess I'd be worried, too, if my, uh, wife were, uh, expecting." He's bright red.

"You big doofus. You gotta aks somebody out first."

"I'm working on it."

He's real sweet, you know? No matter what, he's a good guy. I respect this guy. I trust him. He makes me feel good.

I drag him over to the dance floor, but no way he's gonna dance. So we just watch. Anyways, nobody's dancing except the girls from Payroll mostly with each other and maybe a couple of guys from the mailroom, though a lot of the girls are looking like they'd like to. All the papers are just staying off by themselves, especially those fucking *Skirt* people who keep making these loud comments about how they told everybody they're going to this real exclusive club that's really one of a kind and laughing at everybody else and thinking they're a real riot. Dopes. They're putting me back in a bad mood. Shit. When you're not in love with somebody, nothing's no fun.

Chapter 38

*E*very year there's a fight in the family about Christmas. Who's gonna be where, who's gonna do what. I mean, it ain't worth it. No wonder people kill themselves at the holidays. Who can put up with all the yelling? Lately Jeanette always wants to do Christmas, I think because she figures it ain't real at Pop's house what with Kathy there. But that means we gotta stand around trying to talk to Nick's relatives. That's a thrill. I mean, it ain't nice to say, but when they kick off, nobody's gonna miss 'em.

His mother's a real prize. She'll criticize the way you blow your nose. I mean, this lady don't like nothing. She don't like the way nobody else cooks. "This is okay," she says, "but it's not the way I make it." Like everybody's killing themselves to steal her recipes, like she was some little Italian Julia Child or something. I mean, she don't like the way you carry the goddamn food to the table.

And his father. Forget about it. I don't know if the man knows English or what. All he does is grunt. Really. Like if you tell him a joke, he gives you his laugh grunt. If you tell him something interesting, he gives you his "No kidding?" grunt. You tell him bad news, you get his "What can you do?" grunt. That's it. That's his entire repertoire, as they say.

And that's just his parents. Don't get me started on his brothers. They make Nick look like fucking Prince Philip. So you get the picture.

Anyways, everyone's real touchy this year on account of my being pregnant, and Nick don't want me parading in front of his family, anyways. Like I care what those bastards think.

So Jeannie ain't coming here and we ain't going there. I don't know what's with her. I don't know who appointed her queen bee. I mean, Christmas without your sister! Jesus, what's the point? I wanna be there when the kids open up their presents. Donna wanted Dream House Barbie but I won't buy that shit. *We girls can do anything.* Give me a break. We girls can sit around in our expensive outfits on our thin asses waiting for some Ken doll to make his move. I got her one of those Talking Whiz Kid deals. You know, them things with the microchips in 'em teach kids stuff. And this gorgeous black velveteen dress with an empire waist and red satin ribbons. I'm a little worried about the lint, though. I got Joey Lego blocks, but he'll probably just put 'em in his mouth.

At least Vicky's all excited. She's bringing over all this food like Kathy don't know how to make toast. I told Vicky it was an insult, but she don't get it. "No," she says, "That way she don't have to bother. I'll do all the work." Like we should all kiss her feet or something.

We always celebrated Christmas when we was kids, even when Ma was around. We never did any of that other stuff. You know. Jewish-type stuff. I don't know nothing about it, really. Maybe Ma felt left out or something. I don't remember she ever said anything like that. But I guess that don't mean nothing.

We always got our tree on Christmas Eve and then took it right home and decorated it. So I got it in my head to go meet Pop at the store and help him pick out the tree, you know? Like old times. I don't really know what he told the guys at work, but I don't care, neither. It's his friggin' place, too. What? They never did something not so aiy-yiy-yiy in their lives? Don't give me that. Just aks Ralph how many months after he was married before little Ralph was born. Yeah. He thinks maybe people didn't talk about it all over the neighborhood for years. So he's got a nerve.

I can tell Pop's not real glad to see me when I walk in, but he's gotta face facts. I'm not gonna hide in no back alleys the rest of my life. I just tell the guys, "Merry Christmas," and they do the same and Pop says real quick he's leaving now and gives me the bum's rush out of the store. Then he's gotta go back in 'cause he forgot all the stuff he was supposed to bring home with him. I wait by the door and Mario comes over to me.

"Here, Tina," he says, and presses something into my hand.

"What's this, Mario?" I look. It's an envelope.

"For the baby. For Christmas."

"You didn't have to, Mario."

"You never have to give no present. We wanted to. Me and Ralph. Don't worry, kid. It'll all work out. You're a good kid, anyways."

"Thanks, Mario."

"Times are different."

"I guess so."

Pop pushes me out again, but I ain't even mad.

He sees the envelope. "What's that?" he aks me.

"A present from Ralph and Mario."

"They didn't tell me they was getting you no present." "So?"

"So nothing." But I can tell he's cheered up.

"You gonna open it?"

"Should I wait till tomorrow?"

"Naw. Open it."

In the envelope are two hundred-dollar bills.

"It's a lot, Pop."

He looks like he's gonna cry. "They're okay. They're okay, those guys."

So we walk over to Leopoldi's Hardware where they got

the trees outside, and Pop's in a good mood, joking with everybody and he's not embarrassed no more. Well, if that's what it took.

I choose a real big tree, but Pop says it won't fit, but Mr. Leopoldi says he'll just cut a little off, it'll be fine. Pop aks how much and Mr. Leopoldi says sixty bucks, and Pop gives him a look like is he kidding or what, so then he says, okay, fifty, and Pop shells out the money and the helper ties it up. That's the way it used to be. Me and Jeannie'd pick out the biggest tree and Pop'd say no and then we'd say, "Please, Pop, please," and he'd get it and Ma or Aunt Vicky would say it was too big and who was gonna clean up all them pine needles?

When we get to the house Vicky's already there bossing Kathy around and putting her dishes in the oven and taking Kathy's out, and I'm thinking this is only fucking Christmas Eve. By tomorrow, they'll probably have killed each other. I mean, what it took to convince Vicky she didn't have to cook a twenty-pound turkey at her house and carry it over.

I bought all these new Christmas decorations and Kathy comes over to look at 'em. I got a lot of stuff like teddy bears and rocking horses and shit like that. She starts putting 'em up but I stop her and start tying a ribbon in each of those hanger things first and she gives me a look and I think maybe I'm driving her a little nuts.

"Since when are you so particular?" she aks.

"But it looks nice, Kath."

"Tina, we wanna eat tonight. This'll take forever."

"I want it to look nice."

So she backs off and then even gets into it, and Pop comes in but he don't notice what we're doing, but then Vicky sees us and makes a face.

"Where's all the old decorations?"

"We're using some of 'em."

"I don't see 'em. I don't see the old decorations."

"Here, Aunt Vicky." I point to this Santa Claus been around since the year one with the paint mostly chipped off the glass. "I hung this one right here."

"Well, I don't know why we needed new things. We

always used the old ornaments. No one said nothing to me."

I look at Kathy and she looks away so's not to crack up. "Okay, Aunt Vicky."

" 'Okay,' she says. You hear her, Sal? But she still does want she wants to do."

And that's pretty much the way it's been with me and Aunt Vicky. I go into the bedroom to lie down and call Jeannie. She's busy with the cooking for tomorrow and don't wanna talk. That's what I mean. Christmas gets everybody crazy.

It don't matter what anybody gets me. Jeannie told me Donna made me something in school and whatever it is, that's all I care about. I already framed some of her pictures. Dogs, babies. She's real good, too. I spent a lot on everybody this year. I bought Vicky this necklace. I just figured she's got nobody to buy her that kind of stuff. I mean, I think she went with this guy for a while once. He was a salesman or something for the place where she's a bookkeeper. One of them big lingerie companies over on Seventh Avenue. I don't know what the story was. I mean, something happened. But it was a long time ago.

It's just as well I can't eat too much on account of the heartburn, because what with Vicky and Kathy bumping each other's stuff off the stove everything's either cold or burnt. Then Vicky goes to wash her own dishes like Kathy don't know how to wash 'em. But nobody's mad, really. I'm pretty drunk, 'cause I figure the alcohol can't hurt the baby by now, and just sitting with my hands on my belly like a fat old hen. The bell rings and Pop goes to answer the door, and I don't even notice at first who it is, but then I look up and Vinnie's standing in the living room.

I forget for a minute what's happened and think it's perfectly okay for him to be there, my boyfriend and all on Christmas, but Pop looks real strange and I see behind Vinnie this little blond shrimp and I know that must be Connie.

Vinnie's brought a bottle of something and Pop goes to

open it and I guess it's no hard feelings or something. Old Connie's hanging onto Vinnie's arm and saying, "Ain't you gonna tell 'em, Vinnie?" And Vinnie smiles like something hurts him and he says, "Yeah. I'm gonna tell 'em." And Kathy stands there like she does with her arms hugging herself and aks, "Tell us what?" And this Connie can't keep her mouth shut, says, "That we're getting married. Just thought you'd like to know." And I feel a little weird, but not sad or nothing. Just kind of empty like I don't care but I should. I guess it was real important to them that we knew.

Vicky looks like she's gonna bust a gut, but I gotta hand it to Pop. He calls for a toast, and then we all drink, and Vinnie introduces us all to Connie. She don't look at me, just my stomach, and gives this real mean smile. I guess she thinks I care or something. She reminds me of that little girl in the comic strip. The one with Charlie Brown in it. You know what I mean? Lucy. Connie's the type, she don't know she won unless she's taken points away from somebody else.

They go and we're all quiet and don't know what to say, but Vicky aks do we wanna go to midnight mass, and that changes the subject and we turn on the TV for some music while we get ready to go out.

I haven't been for a few years. I mean, I don't believe in any of that shit, but that don't mean you can't go and look every so often. Vicky insists we go to her church, which means walking about ten blocks on account of Pop don't wanna move the car 'cause he's got a spot through the weekend. We go slow 'cause it's getting hard for me. But I gotta say it's worth it. Inside the place is beautiful. All lit up, and Christmas trees everywhere. They must have twenty, thirty trees all around the church, all with gold ornaments and dark red ribbons. And it smells so good. That incense they use. And the choir is singing, and the candles are burning in red glass holders. And it don't matter what it's about. It's a place of beauty. It's a place of peace. I don't belong, but tonight I'm here with my family.

Chapter 39

Ma's getting better, I guess. They got her on her medicine and they moved her out to this group home. I ain't been too anxious to see her. I mean, I can't be like Jeannie and pretend she ain't there, but it's no use fooling myself she's any kind of mother. Fern says it's a miracle I turned out so well, considering. But you have to figure everybody's got something to deal with, some kind of problem. I mean, you ever meet somebody without no problems? Yeah? It just means they ain't talking.

But this social worker keeps calling me says it's real important Ma has contact with her family, and I pick a day and make myself go out there. I feel bad what with its being New Year's and all and here I am about to have this baby. Everybody says it's gonna be a boy, but I can't figure that. I just can't figure on a boy being inside my body. Stupid, huh? But I mean, I'm a girl. That's what I know.

Anyways, the neighborhood where Ma's place is ain't too bad, lots of apartment buildings still kept up and private houses, too, and I know I'm at the right place because there's this looney-looking guy on the porch just hanging out wearing a short jacket and ski cap and something's wrong with one of his eyes and he's just staying there not moving even though it's pretty cold. I'm happy he don't say nothing to me when I go in.

Inside it's pretty depressing because it don't look like a real house. More like a community center with a desk up front and these people who look like they don't belong nowhere sitting around on couches somebody donated and talking too loud. I aks for Ma and this tall woman with short, curly hair wearing gray pants and a sweater like some gung-ho gym teacher type gives me the room number.

I go up the stairs trying not to bump into anybody and knock on the door. Ma says, "Just a minute," and I catch my breath and start to cry. I ain't heard her sound like that in years. I mean, she sounded, you know, normal. I'm quick wiping away the tears before she opens the door.

She looks pretty good, too. Her hair's still dyed but this time it's some brown color looks okay. And her makeup's not too bad. She's gained weight, but I think that's from the medication. She's wearing clothes out of some shopping bag it looks like, the pants are that polyester crap, but at least they look like they were made in the last ten years or so. Not like that stuff Grandma used to find for her.

She smiles at me and I give her a peck, but I can tell that touching still makes her a little nervous. I sit on this one plastic chair she's got and she sits on the edge of the bed. I see she don't know what to say.

"I'm glad you're better, Ma."

"Yeah, this place is okay."

"Good. You look good."

"Thank you, Tina. You look good, too. That's a pretty dress. You always looked good in that color. What do you call it?"

"Maroon."

"Maroon." She nods like I told her something she's gotta think about for a while.

"The baby's due any week now, Ma."

"Good, Tina."

She don't say nothing so I go on talking. "Jeannie's

getting me all the stuff that goes with the crib, and Ka—uh, somebody else is getting me all the layette stuff. You can order it from the store and they wait till the baby comes so they know whether to send it in pink or blue."

Her head keeps nodding away. I can't tell if she's interested or what, but I keep going. "And at work they're giving me a shower and I think they're gonna chip in on one of them baby carriers or diaper bags or something like that. And then Pop said he'll get me a carriage but I told him I don't need no carriage. You can't get them in and outta stores. And heavy? Forget about it. I want one of them strollers. You know what I mean?"

"Stroller." She nods.

"Pop said he called you, right?"

"Sure. Sal called me. He didn't come to see me, though." Now she's shaking her head.

"Well, it's hard for him."

"He called me, though."

"I know." I'm thinking of things to say. "Jeannie's doing real well. The kids are great. Donna's a whiz in school and Joey's almost walking."

She smiles. "I seen Donna when she was a real baby."

"Yeah. What a beautiful baby. I hope my baby looks like that."

"A real little baby. But I don't remember Joey."

"Well, he's real young, Ma. You got a picture of him?"

"Picture? No."

I take out my wallet and show her the pictures of the kids. She holds each one up close and looks at it for a long time. I explain to her who's who. She likes the one of Donna with Joey, hugging him.

"Keep 'em, Ma. Jeannie'll give me new ones. You should have pictures of the kids."

She smiles. And I'm glad, 'cause I didn't bring her nothing and now at least I gave her this. I mean, what do you bring to someone in a nuthouse?

Anyways, I see it ain't no use trying to say anything to her, but at least she's calmed down. It's funny visiting her here. I mean, when she went away when I was a kid, they never let us go to her.

"It's good to see you, Ma. I hope you're, uh, better when the baby comes so you can come over."

"What?"

"The baby. When my baby's here."

"Oh."

Suddenly I feel the baby kicking inside me. "Look, Ma, you can see her move! Look at my belly!"

But she don't see it. She just sits there smiling at me. I see she's gonna let the pictures of Donna and Joey drop out of her hand, so I take them and prop them against the little mirror on top of this cheap old dresser they gave her. There's a Fuller brush lying there. Jesus. I didn't know they made that stuff anymore.

"Remember when the Fuller brush man used to come around, Ma?"

"Yeah, I remember that. I bought you girls hairbrushes. You had real long hair always got snarls in it. You never would stand still to have your hair brushed. Always a fight with you. You were too much for me."

"I'm sorry, Ma." I feel real sad. I pick up the brush. "Would you like me to brush your hair, Ma?"

"Okay," she says very quiet.

So I go and stand over her and brush her hair real slow and careful. I don't wanna disturb nothing. I don't wanna hurt her.

Chapter 40

Ginny, my Lamaze instructor, just called me here at work to tell me one of the couples in our class already had the baby. You can imagine how I feel. I mean, it's getting close. I'm all excited, so I go to tell Fern, and she's really whooping it up.

Anyways, even that bastard Lynn has to smile and I can tell jerky Gene's feeling all warm and gooey inside. Christ, here's someone thinks he's an okay guy. Thinks he's nice, for godsake. When all the time he's asshole first class.

Sometimes I think I'm gonna miss this place. I know that's stupid, but I tell you, working in an office ain't all that bad. Even when the people are jerks. Really. I mean like now, when everybody's happy. Or when we all stand around and talk about last night's "thirtysomething" or some other program. It's funny how you start to care about the people in a TV show. Like they're people you know. I worry about 'em from one week to the next. Worry they'll do something stupid in between when I'm not watching.

Times like these, this is almost like a real office. You know what I mean? Where you can walk down a hallway and everybody's got their little space, cubicle, whatever, not bunched all together in an open pit of a newsroom. They got their little bulletin boards with photos and cartoons they cut out of magazines and birthday cards stuck on 'em with push pins. And dirty coffee cups sitting on the desks. You know, with the old coffee caked in rings on the bottom. And you stop in and sit on the extra chair and talk about some bullshit and then your boss or somebody passes by and catches you. I mean, all we got is the dirty cups. And if Frieda didn't buy the fucking coffee, we wouldn't have shit. I mean, she once tried to get the guys to chip in for cake. Forget about it.

Maybe that's why it's so hard for some people to leave a job, even when they hate it. I mean, it's like the fucking office becomes part of your family. Like you get all caught up with these morons.

Anyways, it's the right day for the news about the baby 'cause they're giving me this shower. I can tell Lynn is like sick to his stomach that this is happening in old macho land, but too fucking bad. Sometimes I think the guy's unstable, you know? Anyways, I don't let it get to me. But I'm sorry 'cause Ange is out again. I mean, I thought that shit was over with.

Anyways, they got an ice cream cake and wine and everything set up in the conference room and I'm thinking it's Fern done it, but she says no, it's Frieda, and I think maybe she's not so bad. Maybe she's even a little sorry she's been such a bitch the whole time. So I'm feeling good, but then that jerk-off Rochelle comes over all smiley and makes some remark about whose name I'm gonna give the baby 'cause I'm not sure who the father is or some shit like that.

"What kind of crack is that?" I aks her.

"I didn't mean anything, Tina."

"Right."

Then she opens her eyes real wide and says, "Well, if you're gonna be that way about it."

You ever hear the expression "false friend"? You know what I mean? Rochelle's the kind of person, if you was crossing the street together, and a car came at you and you didn't see it but she did, she'd push you in front of her.

But I'm real happy with the Snugli thing they got me to wear the baby right next to me when I walk around and the other shit they bought, and everybody's trying on the Snugli for a joke and eating cake and it's real nice, but then the phone rings and of course it's my extension. Fern's real sweet and she says she'll get it for me. But then she comes back and stands in the door of the room and like signals for me to come and I know something's up.

"Better get it, Tina," she whispers. "It's Angie."

And my throat starts to ache like I swallowed a baseball instead of Carvel. I get on, and it's a little hard to understand her 'cause she's crying so much.

"What's up, Ange? That bastard hurt you again?"

"Oh, Tina, please, just come here."

"Should I call an ambulance?"

"No. They took him already."

"Took who?"

"Jim."

"The police?"

"No, no. The medics. Whatever they are."

"Jesus, Ange, what did you do?"

"No. It's Dommy. My Dommy. Tina, what am I gonna do? You can't tell nobody. I don't want no one to know."

"Ange, please, what happened? Dommy got hurt?"

"No, Jim."

"Dommy hurt Jim?"

"He tried to kill him."

"Holy shit, Ange."

"He was hitting me. I didn't think he was gonna come back, you know? And Dommy was gonna move back in, you know? But then Jimmy started coming over to the house a couple times and I shouldn't of done it but I started fighting with him for walking out and all and he got mad. So this time Dommy . . . Dommy . . . Sweet Jesus, Tina. They took Dommy."

"Ange, where are you?"

"I'm at the hospital. They took me to the Maimonides and they wouldn't let me go with my boy. And Jimmy's in another hospital. I don't know where they took him. Tina, please, you gotta come help me. I can't face nobody. And nobody's telling me nothing."

"Where's Carla?"

"I can't bother her now, Tina. She's at the store. People'll find out. She can't afford to lose her job."

"Oh, Ange." I mean, she's talking crazy. I'm gonna aks her about her other kid, but then I remember he's in the army or something. And I don't think she's got family. I mean, would her father of let her stay with that bum if he'd been around? Unless her father was a bigger bum.

The thing is, I don't feel like going. I mean, the Goodyear blimp got nothing on me. And I'm in the middle of my goddamn party. I feel like a prime piece of shit, too, on account of all the trouble she's in. But Jesus, she brung it on herself. Though I guess this ain't the time for that.

But I got all this shower crap to lug with me. I can't exactly show up at the hospital with a plastic bathtub and a bunch of little outfits. So I'm telling Fern what's up and how I gotta go home first. Everybody's nosing around, especially Frieda and Rochelle who think maybe they'll go into cardiac arrest if ever somebody knows something before they do.

So me and Fern are gonna call a cab, but Yoshi butts in he wants to go, too, and I figure, what the hell? What the hell am I keeping Angie's secrets for anymore? It's probably gonna make the front page of the fucking *Post* tomorrow. I mean, let everybody know. Maybe if somebody would of known, this friggin' thing would never of happened.

Funny thing about Yoshi, too. He always wants to be in on things, but he never really lets himself get involved in what's going on, you know what I mean? Like his feelings are always a little bit off to the side. I don't think it's because he's this weird mix, neither. I mean, most people got a little of this or that in 'em. Look at me. It's just that for such a smart guy, Yoshi don't seem to know what to do sometimes. He can't make the first move. It's not that he can't be nice. It ain't that. I mean, if you aksed him a favor like to crash at his place or have him help you move or something, he'd do it in a minute. But if a big weekend was coming up, he'd wait to aks you out until Saturday afternoon.

So the three of us take a taxi to my place and tell the cabbie to wait while we bring the shower stuff up. Fern and Yoshi both go nuts over the apartment 'cause of how it's been fixed up. I mean, if they'd seen it before they would of thought it was pathetic. But Nick built this three-quarters wall in the hall to make a room for the baby, and he and some of his guys painted the whole place this peach color. I mean, I think he told his crew that my husband was killed in some car accident or something. Really. I mean, he can't handle it.

And then I got a couch in what they call this teal color, and two chairs that don't match exactly but go together. You know what I mean? And I bought all these pillows to put on them, and these old pictures I saw at the flea market of flowers and ladies in old-timey clothes. And this funny rug with fishes on it that's got all the colors in the room. I thought the baby'd like that. You know, crawling around on it. Anyways, I think I spent more on issues of *House Beautiful* than on all the fucking furniture put together.

So I'm telling them about where I got all the stuff and Yoshi goes into the bedroom to look around.

"Tina! A brass bed! I love it!"

And I feel real happy 'cause I know it looks like a home. So we're having a good time, but then we remember we left the cabbie downstairs waiting and we gotta get over to Ange.

Chapter 41

When we walk in, I see Angie at the end of the hall sitting on a bench in the emergency room, her head down, two cops standing next to her. She looks beat. I have this crazy thought like she's the criminal and they're guarding her. I don't know. I guess it's this place, with the friggin' fluorescent lights making everything seem cold, and the smell like somebody just washed the place with Lysol or something, like they was trying to cover up the stink of the world. And the way Ange won't look up at us.

She don't even seem mad I brung Fern and Yoshi. To tell the truth, I don't think she even noticed. I mean, what with the state she's in and all. Even with her head down I can tell she looks real bad. The bastard. I mean, her face is all discolored and puffy and one eye's closed up. Fern had tears in her eyes when she looked at her. I saw.

They've finished treating her, but she's going crazy 'cause she can't see Dommy, so she finally lets me call Carla who's cold as ice. I don't hold it against her. I figure if she wasn't, she wouldn't of made it this far. But she's not a bad person. She says she'll come right over. All she aks about her father is, is he dead yet.

Thing is, Ange wants a lawyer for Dommy and don't know who to get. I mean, she don't want some scumball in some sleazy storefront office who's just used to doing evictions all day. She wants someone big time. I tell her that'll cost her, but she don't care. But we don't know no lawyers. Except, I mean, I know Noah. So I tell her I know somebody who maybe could help and she feels better.

Meanwhile Yoshi finds out they took Jim to King's County, but they won't give us no more information, so Yoshi says he'll go way the hell over there, but I don't think it's such a good idea. I mean, what's he gonna say? That he's a relative? So I aks one of the policeman real nice, and I figure he's a soft touch or maybe it's 'cause I'm pregnant, he walkie-talkies something or other. He tells us Jim's critical.

Fern aks what the hell happened 'cause we still don't know, and the cop tells us Dommy shot Jim. That fucking big macho man kept a gun in his dresser drawer and Dommy knew it, and seems he walks in and sees Jim going after Ange and Dommy runs to get the gun and lets him have it. And then Yoshi aks how many times, 'cause he's a fucking reporter. And this cop, he's real young, says with a smile like he's enjoying it, at least three.

Meanwhile, I aks Ange how come Jim came back, and she tells me the bimbo threw him out. I guess he started getting tough with her. What a laugh. The goddamn whore had her standards.

Ange raises her head a little and I see she also lost some teeth, and what with that and the lawyer I don't know where she thinks she's gonna pay for it all.

Which reminds me about Noah. I don't even know if he's back home or what, but I go again to the public phone and stand in the little booth looking through my bag for his number, it's been so long since I called him, and find a pair of baby booties I threw in there from the shower and start to look at them but then keep going till I find Noah's card on the bottom.

It's already almost six, but the receptionist answers,

though she sounds real put out. I guess everybody's still there. That's how it is in some places. They never wanna go home.

I aks for Mr. Lieb's office.

"Well, is it important?" I don't know why I have to go through this with her all the time.

"Jesus, lady. Would I be calling this late if it wasn't?"

"Well, excuse me. Who is this, please?"

"Ms. Scacciapensieri."

"Oh. Can you spell that?"

"Yeah, I can spell it. But can you?"

"What is that, some kind of joke?"

"Look, just put Noah on, okay?"

I guess I sounded convincing because next thing I hear is Noah's voice. It's funny to hear it after all this time. It sounds different, somehow. I can't even answer for a minute.

"Tina? Is that you? Are you all right?" Then real upset, "Did the baby come already? Oh, shit. I wanted to be there."

"What are you talking about?"

"I wanted to be with you when the baby was born."

"Oh. That's why you went away and I never heard from you for months. I see how bad you wanted it."

"Didn't you get my postcard?"

"Yeah. It was almost like having you there. Really."

"I'm sorry. I just, well. I can't really talk now. But I was doing some work in Milan for one of our clients. And I sort of stayed. But I thought about you so much. I bought you stuff. I bought the baby stuff. Adeena thought I must be the father."

"Oh."

"No, Tina. It's not like that. She was only with me a week or so. She got this modeling thing in Italy. They really go for her looks there."

"Oh don't bother, Noah. I didn't call you for all that. The baby ain't born yet. You didn't miss nothing. I called for a friend. It's a long story, but she needs a lawyer.

Someone real good for her son. He tried to off his old man."

"A friend of yours?"

"Yeah, a friend of mine. Don't your ears work?"

"Okay, okay. But, Tina, you know I'm not a criminal lawyer."

"Noah, I don't know what the fuck kind of lawyer you are, okay? You're a lawyer, right? You know other lawyers? So just give me a name. And don't make him too expensive, you know? I don't know what she can afford."

He kind of laughs and then says he's thinking. Then he aks shit like about what happened and where Dommy is and everything. Then he goes aks somebody something and then comes back and tells me okay, he'll take care of it.

"Thank you. I'll send you an announcement."

"Don't be angry, Tina. I really think about you all the time."

"Yeah?" I says, looking down the hall where Angie is. "Well that don't win no prizes."

Chapter 42

I tell you, it really shook me up talking to Noah. I mean, I thought I'd stop, you know, thinking about him, but it just don't go away. I guess that's how Angie is about Jim. And how Noah is about his wife.

He went back to that Adeena after she treated him like dirt. She thinks she's God's gift, but she don't know shit. A guy like that, whatever his problem, you don't put up for grabs.

So after a while I get to thinking maybe I was a little rough with him on the phone. I mean, the guy don't owe me nothing. It ain't his lookout a crazy half-Italian girl who got herself knocked up kicked over her boyfriend and gave her family a hard time. I would of done it anyways. But I guess I sort of thought he was setting something up, if you see what I mean.

So I'm thinking I should call him. I mean, thank him for getting that lawyer for Dommy. Seems it's some lady, and Dommy likes her real well. Ange says she guesses the woman knows what she's doing, but I think Ange would of preferred a man. Go figure.

Meanwhile, I gotta give Frieda instructions for whoever's

175

gonna do my work while I'm out. That's a conversation I'm really looking forward to, let me tell you. I mean, this is just the kind of stuff she gets off on. But I don't get so upset no more. I mean, I know her sad tale. And after the shower and all, who can get mad?

They're gonna divvy up the job between a few people, maybe get a temp in if it ever gets real busy. So Frieda's pissed 'cause it's gonna mean more work for her. But she's been with the place fifteen years. She should know that if there's a cheap way of doing something, they'll do it.

Fern's been sending out résumés. She's ready to jump ship. She's been working her business contacts, too, but that's been pretty discouraging. No one really wants to help you. Like it's skin off their teeth if you had a job, too. I think, with some people, the minute you need something, they freeze up. They forget how to be people. It's like you're trying to take something away from them.

But Tony's caught on that Fern's gonna leave and that kind of woke him up. He aks do I think he should, too. "What are you aksing me?" I tell him. "Don't you know?" He rolls his eyes like I went too far, but that just gets me crazy. "Oh, grow up, Tony." He walks away like he's real mad, but I know he wanted me to yell at him. It worked, too, because next thing I hear him aksing Fern to lunch.

Then stupid Rochelle comes over to aks me what's with Fern and Yoshi. She's always a couple of steps behind. I don't tell her shit. What's it her business? She just aksed 'cause she don't like it he don't pay no attention to her. "I don't get it," she says. "What could they possibly have in common?" I just look at her cross-eyed. Makes me miss Ange, too. That's the kind of thing we always got on about.

Ange's home now, but Dommy's back with Carla, out on bail. It broke Ange's heart he wouldn't live with her. I'm begging her to come back to work. Jim's still in the hospital. Something got severed and they think he's gonna be paralyzed. And I say good. I say, let the bastard suffer. Let the bastard sit in a wheelchair the rest of his miserable life and think about what he done.

I just don't know what this whole thing's gonna do to Dominick. Although let's face it. The kid obviously wasn't dealing from a full deck before any of this happened.

Why is it so many people get fucked up? You know any normal people? Yeah? I don't think so.

Chapter 43

When I get home I call Jeanette and Kathy to let them know nothing's up with the baby yet, even though I'm two days from my due date. I got a number where to reach Fern. I feel like I'm out on probation, or something, I gotta check in with so many people.

I'm beat, and the weird thing is I feel like I got cramps. I'm lying there thinking about Noah and start rubbing my hands over my breasts, which are so full now. I'm driving myself crazy and touch myself soft because that's all I need and I'm worried maybe I shouldn't be doing it at all. But I think about his body, I think about him inside of me, shit, I can't help it. Besides, it always helps with cramps.

But the cramps are still bad and now I'm thinking maybe this is it. Then I'm thinking what is all the fuss about if labor is just like having your period? But I don't wanna be a jerk and call the doctor. Maybe it's false labor. I call Jeanette back to aks what she thinks.

"If it don't hurt too much, it ain't it," she says.

"Oh. I thought maybe it was."

"It's no goddamn picnic, Tina. It took me two days to deliver Donna. You remember."

"Yeah, I guess so." I'm not really listening 'cause now I think I'm feeling something else.

"Jeannie, it's starting to really hurt."

"Then that's it."

"Jesus, I'm scared."

"Well, I'd be scared too if I was there by myself."

"Come on, Jeannie. I'm gonna call Fern. She'll come right over."

"Right. Fern."

"Jeannie!"

"Okay. Look. Don't panic. You got plenty of time, okay? Get someone over there. I'll call in an hour. And don't forget to call the doctor, okay? You okay?"

I let out a breath. "Yeah, I'm okay. I'm gonna call Fern now."

"Go call Fern."

Thing is, Fern ain't home, which I didn't tell Jeanette. She's out with Yoshi, but I got the number of the restaurant. It's not even seven o'clock, so I know I'm ruining their dinner, but what the fuck.

I call, but they ain't there. I try Fern's place. No answer. And I realize like a dope I don't have Yoshi's number. I'm going crazy. I'm okay between contractions, but when they come I don't know what to do. It's like someone's punching me right up through the middle till my whole body aches. You can't stand and you can't sit. I can't remember how to do the breathing. I'm crying and grab the phone to call Kathy.

Pop answers. "What's wrong, Tina? Is it the baby?"

But I don't wanna talk to him. "I need Kathy," I tell him. Too bad if it hurts his feelings.

I hear Kathy yelling at him. Then she's on the phone. "What's wrong? You okay?"

I feel like I'm two years old. "I can't find Fern," I'm sobbing. "Could you come over, please, Kath? Right now?"

"I'm out the door."

So then I cut the crying and get my hospital stuff together. I'm deciding whether or not to eat this Jell-O they tell you to have ready in case you're hungry and you can't have no big meal or nothing, because really I hate Jell-O, when the phone rings. It's Fern and I practically take her head off.

"Where are you?"

"Take it easy, Tina." She kind of whispers. "We just got to the restaurant. We stopped off at Yoshi's first."

"What?"

She whispers louder. "We went to Yoshi's place before the restaurant."

She sounds weird and at first I don't get it.

"Great," I tell her. "I'm having this fucking baby and you and Yoshi are fucking around."

"The baby! The baby's coming? Oh, Tina, I'm sorry! You okay? When did it start?"

"Just can the questions and get the hell over here."

Meanwhile Kathy shows up and I never been so glad to see nobody in my whole life. I aks her to help me shower and she's a little shy about it, but it don't bother me. The water feels nice. It feels good to have someone there to help me in and out, just like I was a little kid. Someone to dry me and get me dressed. She looks at all the Lamaze stuff I'm taking, like the champagne and lollipops and tennis balls. She thinks it's funny and just starts laughing her head off, and then Fern and Yoshi get there and Jeanette calls and it's like there's a party going on here or something.

Fern does the breathing with me and times the contractions at five minutes apart. She calls Bliss, but he says wait and I'm sorry 'cause I'm really scared. So we hang out and then the contractions are coming closer, about every three minutes, and Fern calls again and this time he says come in. By now it hurts so much I can't think and I can hardly walk. We go outside and I see it's starting to snow, that magic nighttime kind, where the air is soft and the flakes fall real slow and they make the street sparkle. Fern and Yoshi kind of drag me to the car. I get in back with Fern and Kathy gets up front with Yoshi, and even the way I feel I can see she's blushing 'cause he's so cute. Yoshi drives real slow and keeps aksing am I all right.

I'm pressing Fern's hands and praying there's no traffic 'cause Yoshi's car's a mess and I don't wanna have my baby on top of a bunch of old maps and a softball glove and loose change and dirty rags. Yoshi turns on the radio to one of those oldie stations and it's John Lennon singing "Beautiful Boy" and we all get quiet and sad and Fern says when it's through that she never got over John's being killed like that.

So we're all thinking about that and it's like I'm in two different places: here in the car and then in the pain. And it's funny, 'cause I still can't really believe that the baby's coming. That all this is because the baby will be here in a little while.

We pull up to the hospital and Fern and Kathy haul me out of the car and over to Admissions, and the nurse is probably blind or something because she don't even aks do I wanna sit, just aks me all about my insurance. Fern gets all annoyed and tells her they can keep the baby for security if I try to skip out without paying, but the bitch don't think that's too funny.

Then another nurse says only one person can go with me and Kathy looks upset and I'm real sad 'cause I want her with me, but she goes and Fern changes into a hospital gown and they take me into a labor room. I get out of my clothes and some young resident examines me and he's all nervous and I pray Bliss gets there 'cause this guy looks like he's never seen a woman before, much less a pregnant one. And I aks him what's the story and he says I'm only three centimeters dilated and I know I got a ways to go.

Then Fern comes back and tries to get me to do the breathing and massages me and puts a cool washcloth on my forehead and I just wanna hold on to her for dear life. The nurse aks do I have to go to the bathroom and I says I don't know. But I get up and manage to sit on the pot, all the time staring at this sign they put up in Spanish and English telling you not to flush sanitary pads down the toilet, and I'm thinking, this is the kind of shit I'm gonna remember about having this baby.

Meanwhile, Bliss finally shows up and is falling over

himself apologizing that the birthing room isn't free. And I tell him I don't care. I can't worry about that shit now. I mean, it feels like what I always thought those old-time torture chamber things would be like, you know, when you see them in the movies. And I'm wondering how anyone ever has more than one kid.

He says I'm doing real good but they strap one of those monitor things on me anyways, and that's so uncomfortable but they're checking on the baby so what can I say? And the little resident looks real relieved that Bliss is there although I bet Fern and the nurse could of delivered the baby between them. The nurse is chatting away about how she was a midwife in Jamaica and London so I figure I'm okay.

Fern tells me Yoshi and Kathy are in the waiting room and that Pop's on his way and it makes me feel safe. Then I aks Fern would she call Noah after the baby comes and she gives me a funny look but says yeah.

I feel like a dishrag that's been squeezed and squeezed till it's dry. I mean, that must be what I look like. Then just to take my mind off it I aks Fern what happened with her and Yoshi and she laughs and blushes 'cause everybody's in the room and says, "Nothing much."

"Nothing much because you can't talk about it or nothing much really?"

"Well, something much, but I guess it was probably nothing much."

And she kind of makes a face and I think again that with a guy like Yoshi it's never anything much and maybe it took actually sleeping with him to make Fern finally realize it.

She aks how I'm doing and I say okay. "How are *you* doing, Fern?"

"Pretty good. You've got the hard job."

"But is it hard for you?" I'm thinking about the baby she lost.

"No. Not really. I'm here for you, Tina."

"Yeah, and after I spoiled your date and all."

And she's about to say something but then I grab on to her with all my might because something's happening, something's different. I feel like some cartoon character, like that Wile E. Coyote when the Road Runner shoots a bomb or something straight into his mouth and you see it ram through him and smack up against his insides. And then I realize it's the pushing, that it's really the baby, and they're wheeling me into delivery.

They got most of the lights dim, with like a spotlight on the table, and it's real pretty. Like in a romantic restaurant. There's the doctor and resident and Fern and a couple of nurses and I'm glad so many people are here to greet my child. Then they lug me onto the table and put my feet in the stirrups and I forget how to push, just make these grunting sounds, but Fern calms me down. And I push and then Fern says she can see it, she can see the head, and I can make it out a little in the mirror, and Bliss says the baby's crowning just one more push, and I feel the baby slide out and I'm waiting to hear a boy or a girl but one of the nurses says, "Oh, his arm!" And I don't know what's going on but I hear the baby cry and Fern crying and the resident grasps my shoulder and Bliss says real flat, "Congratulations, Tina, it's a boy. We're just going to clean him up and weigh him and give him his Apgar." And I think: Oh, a boy. But I'm glad. And I say, "Can't I hold my baby?" And Bliss says, "Of course, as soon as he's ready." And then they're sewing me up and I'm shaking and I'm trying to look over my shoulder to where they're bathing him and stuff and the nurse calls out, "Seven pounds, six ounces, nineteen inches," and Fern is holding my hand and I aks her what is it, but she won't say nothing and then they hand me my baby all wrapped up and he's beautiful. I can't believe I'm finally holding my baby. His little face is all squished together and he's all red and his head is a little pointy. He's got a little bit of dark hair and he's like this neat little package. He feels so good.

But then they take him back and Bliss says the baby's gotta go to the nursery to be examined. And they wheel me into recovery and Fern is like wiping her nose and now I'm mad and I aks her what the fuck is going on.

She looks at me real hard and takes a long breath. "There's some problem with his arm, Tina."

"What do you mean? What arm?"

She thinks for a minute. "His right, I think."

"What's wrong with it?"

She shakes her head and speaks so soft it takes me a second before I realize I've heard her.

"I don't know. It's too short and all bent up. I didn't see it all that well."

"Maybe it's just like that 'cause of the delivery or something."

"I don't think so, Tina. I mean, the nurses and everybody, they knew something was pretty wrong."

"Oh." I won't believe this. "I guess they can fix it."

"Oh, I'm sure. It's pretty amazing what they can do these days. You know, microsurgery and all that sort of thing."

I don't know, but I figure maybe Fern does. I keep saying to myself: *Something's wrong with my baby. Something's wrong with my baby.*

Fern gives me her hand and I squeeze it, and we're both crying and I'm like trying to make time go backwards in my mind so that it didn't happen, so that he hasn't been born yet and I can change it.

"I gotta see him, Fern. Tell them I gotta see him. What did they think, if they didn't tell me I wouldn't notice?"

"I think they just wanted to give you time to prepare yourself."

"Yeah? Like how am I supposed to do that? I mean, I guess I know what they was thinking, but I can't prepare myself until I see how bad it is."

She sits down and I can see she's exhausted. I remember she never had no dinner and she's been on her feet for like seven hours. I tell her to go get something to eat.

"I'm not hungry."

"Really?" I'm glad she's not going. "Then let's have the champagne, okay?"

"You sure, Tina?"

I can still see his little face. "Yeah. He's beautiful, ain't he, Fern? You saw him."

"He's beautiful, Tina."

So she goes out for some paper cups and brings them back and the two of us in that little brown room with turquoise chairs toast the birth of my first son.

Chapter 44

*E*verybody's been told about the baby's arm before they come to see me, so they got these real bright smiles on when they walk into my room. Except Pop, 'cause he's too shaken up and can't pretend shit. He aks me what went wrong and I tell him no one knows.

Anyways, that's what the pediatrician told me. She came to see me before they brought the baby back. These things happen, she says. She aksed a lot of questions about did anyone else in the family ever have this condition and about the pregnancy and I started worrying what it was I did to fuck things up. She said it wasn't anything I did. And I thought maybe when I had some wine or beer early on and she said that couldn't of done it. I told her I didn't take nothing the whole time. Not one fucking Tylenol. And she just shrugged and said you can't control something like this and we'd have to discuss the treatment, but I was lucky because he seemed to be normal in every other way, but they'd have to watch him real close and give him all these tests.

I guess I seemed pretty upset, 'cause they aksed if I wanted a private room, but I told 'em my insurance don't pay for no private room, and I ain't gonna start out being ashamed of him, anyways. And then this nurse gets all huffy and says that's not what she meant, but the hell it ain't.

Everybody's bothering me to give him a name. "What's he going to be?" Fern aks. "Baby boy Scacciapensieri?" But I got no ideas. I mean, I was so sure it was gonna be a girl and all. And now . . . But I'm dying to see him.

They make Pop and Kathy put on these yellow gown things before they bring in the babies like they're some kind of tiny royalty or something. The nurse carries him over to me still all swaddled. And Pop glances at him quick and I tell him, "Pop, I'm gonna look at him now."

"No one's stopping you."

Kathy shoots him a look but I don't know what it means. I can't be bothered, you know? It's just them two now, 'cause Yoshi took Fern home to get some sleep and Jeanette hasn't shown up yet. Kathy gets up and pulls closed the curtain they got around the bed and I don't say not to.

He's so little and dear. He's asleep, and I'm careful and slow peeling off the blanket but he stirs anyway and is getting ready to cry. I wanna try to nurse him, but I gotta look at him first.

And it's true. His arm looks like a little wing or something, bent up toward his body. Like it's broken, like when a little bird gets hurt in the street or something. And you walk by 'cause you don't know if it's dead or what and you wouldn't know what to do anyways. *Ladybird, ladybird, fly away home.* And the hand don't look right, and I get this crazy idea like someone stuck the wrong part on. Like he was a toy or something and going down the assembly line someone goofed. Or like he's a puzzle someone put together wrong.

I look up at Pop and Kathy and they're like hanging on to each other, so I rewrap him best I can and put him to my breast. It takes him a minute to quiet down and get the nipple in his mouth, and I gotta scoot around some to get in the right position, and it ain't too easy 'cause my bottom burns like hell, but then it seems to work all right and I feel this delicate little pulling that sort of hurts but sort of feels good and I feel pretty proud of myself 'cause I never done it before or nothing.

By now Pop and Kathy have calmed down and Pop's like embarrassed and kind of turns away, but Kathy leans over me and starts saying a little loud how beautiful he is and how hungry he must be and we're like that when I see a pair of pants legs under the curtain and hear someone calling, "Tina?" Kathy peeks out and then in walks Noah with a gown over his suit and carrying all these boxes and flowers sitting on top of them.

Pop and Kathy look at him like where did he come from? My heart's pounding so hard I can't beathe. He kisses me and looks at the baby and strokes his forehead. And then a nurse comes in and says, "Only two visitors when the babies are out," and Kathy gives me a quick smile and then she and Pop leave.

"God, look at you," he says.

"What? I look like shit, right?"

"No. You look like somebody's mother."

I'm just staring at him, he looks so good. He's watching the baby not saying nothing.

"What did you bring me?" I finally aks.

"All sorts of stuff. For the baby, too."

"I'm glad you came. Did Fern call you?"

"Yes."

"Did she tell you?"

"Yes. I'm sorry, Tina."

"Well, I guess I'm not surprised."

"What do you mean?"

"Something wrong. Something missing. We're a family of misfits."

"Tina!"

"Well, you can think what you like, Noah. I deserved it. I fucked up."

"It wasn't you, Tina."

"Who the hell else was it then?" I'm getting pretty hysterical.

"Nobody. It was nobody."

"Well, something had to be wrong with me or this never would of happened."

He gives me this sharp look. "Don't you feel bad about yourself, Tina. It's the luck of the draw. You did nothing wrong and you are nothing wrong."

"Yeah, sure."

"Look, Tina. This has nothing to do with the kind of person you are or how you live your life. These things happen. I'm sure they told you that. There's no one to blame, certainly not yourself."

"I can't help it."

"Tina, please, little darling," he says and he's kissing me. "I'll help you. I mean, whatever can be done."

"Oh, Noah. I don't know what that means coming from you. I don't know if you're gonna be around or what. Because I need you. I need somebody. He's gonna have to have all these operations and be going to doctors all the time. I don't know how I can do it."

"You'll be fine. You'll be fine," he says with his arm around me. "But let me try to help, okay? Is that okay with you?"

Now I'm crying like a little dope. "I got no right to aks you anything. And don't feel you need to do no penance just 'cause you went to Europe for a couple of months."

"It's not that."

"Maybe."

He collapses next to me on the bed like this conversation's knocking the shit right out of him. "Look, Tina, I don't know what's going on. I can't tell you more than that." He keeps talking to me but looking at the baby. "I want to stick around you and the baby. And we'll see what happens, okay?"

"I don't know. I don't know if that's okay."

"Tina, look, I'm doing the best I can here."

"Fuck you, Noah, you think that's an excuse? That's what we're all doing."

We sit quiet for a minute, me blowing my nose, and I guess there's nothing more to say about it. I watch the baby drift off. I can't get over how little he is. Then Noah aks if he can hold him and I say sure.

He takes him, real tense but so softly. "Is it really bad, Tina?"

"It's really bad."

He pulls down the blanket and looks at the little arm. "Oh my God."

"You want me to take him back?"

"No. No. I'm okay." But he's crying. "Poor darling, poor little darling."

Then I let go again, and I'm sobbing like I'll never stop and I don't give a shit who hears me. But the two of us make such a noise the baby wakes up and I hold out my arms to take him and Noah kisses him and hands him back.

I rock him very gently and talk to him and he quiets down. Noah smiles at me. "You look like you know what you're doing."

"Well, you gotta hold a baby securely. It makes 'em feel safe."

"Okay, Dr. Spock."

"Hey, it's true."

"I believe you."

Then a nurse comes barging in like she didn't notice the curtain was drawn and she gives Noah a look like what is this guy doing sitting on the bed, and she's got this form for the birth certificate and aks me again what's the name. I tell her to come back and she makes a face. I mean, you can't throw them off schedule. It's like they set up this system in a hospital, and they're all fired up to do their routine, and then they look around and there's all these sick people getting in their way.

Noah butts in and aks real sweet if she could just aks the other women first, and she lets out a breath and says okay like she's thought it over and decided to do him this incredible favor. Then he turns back to me.

"Okay, Tina, what's it going to be?"

"You got any ideas?"

"Didn't you have any names picked out?"

"Only for girls."

"Chances were fifty-fifty."

"I know. I just couldn't imagine having a boy. You know, having a little penis growing inside me."

"Oh really? I think I can imagine that."

"Oh, Noah, don't talk dirty now. I can't do nothing about it."

"I can wait." He gives me a smile that I could live on for a month.

"We were talking about a name for this one."

"Well, it's customary to name kids after dead relatives."

"You mean for Jewish people."

"Yes, I mean for Jews."

"But I'm not really Jewish."

"But you are if your mother was, uh, is, Jewish."

"I guess."

"Well, it's just a suggestion."

"No. I like the idea. Except who? I guess there was my grandfather, but he walked out a long time ago, so I don't think he deserves any honors, you know? And there's my grandmother, but I don't really wanna name my kid after her. I mean, she took care of Ma and all, and she was my grandma and all, but she wasn't really such a nice person, if you know what I mean."

"What was her name?"

"Hilda."

"Oh. Anyone else?"

"Not really."

"Well, it could be someone from the other side of the family, or some aunt or uncle, third cousin, anyone."

And suddenly I realize what I'm gonna do.

"There was a baby, I don't know, it would have to be like fifty years ago. A little boy my grandmother lost. He was just a few months old."

"What was his name?"

I have to think for a minute. "Nathan."

"That's not bad."

"You think? Just hand me my name book, okay? It's in the drawer."

He gives it to me and I look up Nathan. "A gift." My eye skips down to the next entry. "Nathaniel: A gift of God."

"Okay," I say showing it to Noah. "Let's go with that."

"Nathaniel," he says and nods. "I'll tell the nurse."

Chapter 45

No wonder they offer you sleeping pills here. There's no chance you're gonna fall asleep. They leave lights on all over the place, and all night people are marching up and down the hall talking and laughing and banging stuff like they waited all day to let loose. Then the lady catty-corner from me aks for her baby for the 1:00 A.M. feeding while all the rest of us didn't, so we hear them bring in her kid and the kid crying, but then it turns out it don't matter 'cause they bring Nathaniel to me anyways.

I don't say nothing 'cause I figure it wasn't no mistake. They just don't wanna hold him. Don't tell me I made it up, neither. But I'm glad, 'cause he nurses like a champ and I'm up anyways and I feel like he's getting to know me.

In the morning I'm waiting for Jeanette to show up. I'm a little ticked off she stayed away yesterday, but she promised to come with Donna today so I guess it's all right. Although I'm not sure how Donna's gonna take this whole thing.

Around eleven I hear them in the hallway. Donna's a

piss. They must be looking at the babies through the window 'cause I hear Donna call out real loud, like she don't notice she's in a hospital, "That's it, Mommy! That's him! I can read the card. It says Scacciapens. They left out some of the letters. His arm don't look so bad from here."

I hear Jeannie shushing her and I swing myself out of bed to go meet them. Donna's up on a chair, looking through the window, an enormous Snoopy doll under her arm. Jeanette turns to kiss me, and I can tell she's upset.

"I told her to be quiet, but she don't listen."

"It's okay, Jeannie, nobody really minds."

"She should know how to behave better."

"It's okay, Jean."

I go up to Donna and give her a kiss. "Hi, Aunt Tina!" she says. "How come you got the broken baby?"

"Donna!" Jeannie says all mad.

"He's not broken, Donna," I says. "Just something wrong with his arm. He was born like that."

"When they gonna fix it?"

"Well, not for a while."

"You still gonna take him?"

"Of course, honey."

"Oh. I don't see why you're gonna take a broken one."

"Just forget it, Donna," Jean says. "Give Aunt Tina the present."

"Oh. Here, Aunt Tina," she says, holding out the Snoopy. He's wearing a sweater and ski cap. "We got this for your baby. I really want to keep it, but I know I can't."

Jeanette lets out a sigh. "Donna!"

"Okay, okay."

"Thanks, honey. Nathaniel'll love it."

"Who's Nathaniel?"

"The baby."

"Where'd you get that from?" Jeannie aks me.

"Why?" I says. "You don't like it?"

"It's just that maybe you should name him something that don't stand out, if you know what I mean."

"Like what?"

"I don't know. Like Frank or Paul or something. Look, just forget it. I shouldn't of said nothing. The name's the least of it. It's fine. I like it." But she sounds like she don't like nothing much. I decide to change the subject.

"How's school, Donna?"

"I hate it."

"You don't hate school," Jeanette tells her.

"Okay. But I hate Miss Petit."

"Who's Miss Petit?"

"She teaches cluster."

"What the hell is that?"

"I mean she is a cluster. We just have her once a week. She's not our real teacher. She's boring."

"What does she teach you?"

"Nothing. She gives us words to copy."

"What words?"

"Stupid words."

"Is that why you hate her?"

"Naw. I hate her 'cause she don't let us go to the bathroom."

"Why don't she let you go to the bathroom?"

"Because she's mean."

"She sounds mean."

"Yeah. She wouldn't even let Andrew go to the bathroom and he's moving to Texas. She didn't even feel sorry for him."

"Well, I guess there are some not nice people in the world."

"Yeah. Let's talk some more about how much we hate Miss Petit."

Jeanette is shaking her head. "Aunt Tina don't wanna hear no more about Miss Petit, Donna." She turns to me. "I shouldn't of brung her."

"Oh, Jeannie, of course you should of."

I see she can't hold it in no longer. "Come here," she says. And I go over and she hugs me tight and the two of us stand there crying. "Oh, Tina," she keeps saying, but I don't say nothing. It feels good just to hold on to her.

Suddenly she breaks away. "I gotta go, Teen. I'm taking Donna to a birthday party."

"But you just got here, Jeannie. Please."

But she won't listen. Donna wants to see Nathaniel up close, so I quick take him out of the nursery and put a blanket around him and sneak over to her 'cause they don't let kids get near the babies.

"Oh, he's so cute. Can I hold him, Aunt Tina?"

"Not this time, honey. Wait till I'm home with him."

Jeannie's tapping her foot. "Come on, Donna, you're gonna be late."

"Don't you wanna see him, Mommy?"

"There'll be plenty of time for that."

I put the baby back and walk them to the elevator. I don't move for a while after they get on and the door closes.

I go back down the hall and look at all the babies sleeping or crying in their bassinets. It's true. From here you can't tell nothing's wrong. And then I pretend everything's okay, or that maybe one of the others is mine.

I move over to the window and stare down. I can see a little inch of river flowing between the white brick of the buildings. It looks real windy and cold outside. Then this tugboat comes chugging along, like straight out of the Golden Book. Scuffy or Tuffy. Scruffy. Something like that.

I get back into bed and don't feel like doing nothing. The other women don't know what to say to me and I don't bother with 'em.

I pick up a magazine but don't know what I'm reading. Then all of a sudden there's a commotion in the hall. I hear this whiny woman's voice saying, "I told you not to come, Vinnie. Now just leave it at the desk and let's go." It takes me a minute to realize it's Connie and Vinnie.

It's like I'm so surprised they're here I don't even think about how weird it is or nothing. I'm lying here waiting for them to come in, but they must of stopped to look at the babies, 'cause the next thing I'm hearing is Vinnie aks, "Can you see anything?"

"Naw. They got him covered up. Good thing, too."

And it ain't like I'm mad, but I just wanna pick up my baby and get him away from her. I push myself out of bed and suddenly in the doorway there's Vinnie, holding something out to me.

"Here, Tina. I can't stay. I wanted to give you something for the baby, you know? For old time's sake. But Connie's outside."

"Yeah. I thought maybe I heard her." I look at the money in his hand but don't move to take it.

"I wanted to see the kid."

"So now you seen him."

He don't say anything, just looks at me hard the way he does trying to figure things out. "Here, just take it," he says, finally, coming nearer. "Please, Tina."

"You didn't have to."

"I know. But I can give a present, even though, you know."

"Yeah, Vin. I'm sorry for everything."

"No." He blushes bright red. "I mean, even if he ain't mine."

"What?"

"I mean, come on, Tina, now it's obvious he can't be mine. No kid of mine could of been born defective."

I feel like I'm gonna faint. I just look at him.

"So just take the money, okay?" he says, trying to press it into my hand.

I open my palm, but don't take it and the bills fall to the floor. We both stand there looking at them. I would of spit at it, too, if it wasn't a hospital.

Vinnie's almost crying. "What is wrong with you, Tina? Even my money ain't good enough for you?"

"Hey, Vin. Just go, okay? And good luck with that Connie."

"What does that mean?"

"Just what it says."

He starts to say something, but don't. He bends down and picks up the dollars.

"Well, see you around, Vin."

"Yeah, see you around." I watch him go down the hall toward Connie.

I wait to make sure they've left and I walk into the nursery to get Nathaniel. He's asleep like nothing's the matter and I pick him up soft and don't disturb him. I sit down slowly in the rocking chair kind of on my side so my bottom don't hurt so much.

Pop comes around then looking for me and just sort of stands there for a while. When he talks it's real low so's not to disturb the baby.

"Was that Vinnie?"

"Yeah. You know it was."

Then he don't speak again for a few minutes.

"You know your aunt Vicky's real upset about this."

"Oh yeah? I noticed she hasn't exactly shown up."

"Well, it's hard on her."

"Sorry to hear it."

He looks annoyed, but lets it pass.

"So what do they say?"

"The doctors? You know what they said, Pop. No one knows why this kind of thing happens."

"I mean about fixing it."

"You sound like Donna."

"Don't give me that, Tina." His voice gets louder. "Why is everything a fight with you?"

I look at him. Poor Pop.

"Sorry."

"Look, if you don't wanna talk about it."

"No, Pop. I gotta talk about it."

"So?"

"So they can operate when he's a little older. Try to straighten it out. And do therapy, exercises or something like that. Even make it so he can use the, uh, hand a little."

"Oh. That ain't too bad."

"No, but Pop, the bone that's supposed to be there ain't there."

"Oh."

"I mean, they can do a lot. But there's a lot of other stuff that might be wrong with him. His kidneys, bladder. Maybe even his heart or blood."

He looks real scared. "Nothing that could kill him?"

"Oh, no, Pop. Not that bad. But, you know, they can never make his arm look exactly right. It'll always be shorter. And they'll have to make him a thumb."

"I see." He nods and turns away. He looks a long time at the glass cabinets with all the formula stacked inside. "Nothing ever like it in my family."

I feel like crying but I don't. "There is now, Pop."

He takes in a breath, walks over, and pats my shoulder. "It's okay, honey. It'll be okay." He plants a long kiss on the top of my head. "Okay, Tina, I'm gonna go now."

We can't look at each other.

"Sure, Pop."

I look down at Natey. He's still napping. The chair is hard but I sit and watch him. I love to watch him sleep. And it's funny, it don't make no sense, but, holding him, I'm thinking that now, even though things went so wrong, or maybe even a little because of it, I feel not so much like I am a mother, but like I have one.

Chapter 46

Fern shows up the next day with Tony just as Kathy and Pop come to help me take the baby home. I mean, Tony called and all, but he managed to wait until the last minute to actually get here. I guess he needed to pull himself together.

Fern chatters away to Kathy and sort of waltzes around poking her head everywhere as if there was a lot of interesting stuff to look at. I mean, four beds, four women in bathrobes, four chairs, a lot of linoleum. Then she spends all this time admiring the flowers the office sent—this weird arrangement probably Frieda picked out with one of them flowers that's got a big long red thing sticking out at you like a prick.

Tony brought this really cute little outfit with bears in sailor suits dancing all over it that Fern helped him choose, and when I look at it lying flat in the box with the two little sleeves folded over each other it makes me feel sad.

The nurse brings in Natey and the thin blanket kind of hangs down away from him and Fern turns her head but Tony smiles. "I guess he's a lefty, huh?"

"Yeah," Pop says, looking away from the window. "A southpaw."

"Right," I says. "The Southpaw."

No one knows what to say after that. But then Fern comes over and aks do I wanna try on the outfit and bring the baby home in it. And I says good idea, because I hadn't thought about that too much and so I change his little diaper and the nurse says we can keep the undershirt they already got on him and then me and Fern try to get these clothes on him and of course they're too big even though they're a small and it takes us awhile to fit the top around his bent arm and then there's all this material left over with nothing in it.

Kathy kind of looks on as we're doing this and sees the trouble and she suddenly starts saying in this singsong, "Nathaniel's arm is spoi-eled, Nathaniel's arm is spoi-eled," and I pretend I don't hear and so does everyone else except Pop who says real soft and kind, "Kathy?" and then she stops.

I mean, I'm not mad or nothing. I can't even bother about that. I mean, she's entitled to be human.

The pediatrician comes up and she gives me the name of someone to see at the hospital in a week, and she smiles and squeezes my arm and tells me everything's gonna be just fine. I think she's just trying to make nice and rush out of here 'cause she don't wanna think about it no more. "You're gonna be okay," she tells me. "You can handle it, I can tell." Yeah. I bet she's glad she don't have to.

When she leaves, Fern's going on and on about what a nice doctor she is, and I can't take it so I says, "Sure. It's easy for her to be nice. I'm taking him home. She never has to see him again. He ain't her kid."

Fern don't know what to say, but Tony comes up to me slowly with this crazy smile on his face like he's doing some comedy routine. He puts his arm around me. "Come on, Tina. Lighten up."

I don't know what's so funny, but I'm cracking up. Fern laughs so hard she's gotta get up and take a piss. Everyone in the room is like looking at us and trying not to smile because they know it ain't funny.

So I'm going home with my baby. It don't feel exactly like I thought it would 'cause I have to keep taking him to see all these other doctors to make sure nothing else is wrong with him as if this wasn't enough, but I feel like once we're home maybe it'll all seem more normal or something and like I just gotta get started.

Fern comes over. "You okay, Tina?"

"Yeah. I was just thinking. It's funny, you know? Before he was born I thought I knew what I was doing, making up my mind in spite of everybody—not that you wasn't behind me from the start—and all the time my little baby was inside me with a messed-up arm. I mean, it makes me feel like I thought I was in one movie when really I was in another completely different one. Like I really didn't know what the fuck was going on and I was acting all the time like I did. I feel like a little dope."

"You're no dope, Tina. No one can control these things."

"Yeah. Ain't that a kick in the head."

She laughs. "Look, kid, Tony and I are gonna go. We'll see you at home in a few days."

I raise my eyebrows. "Tony and I?" I says, mocking her. "*We'll* see you? What the hell is this? Things seem to be pretty okay, huh?"

She looks over to Tony. "Ask him. For my part, I'm not making any promises."

Chapter 47

Well it don't seem fair."

Good ol' Ange. She seems pretty much back to herself. I mean, I don't think she ever really solved nothing, but what with Jim in a wheelchair and helpless as a baby and so no more trouble in that department, and Dommy's lawyer thinking it looks real good for probation, she's picking up the pieces. I mean, let's face it, her life was always a mess. Of course I don't say that to her face. I don't wanna insult her or nothing. But some people just need to be in some kind of trouble to know they're alive.

I shouldn't be too mean, because with all that's going on with her she's still real upset about little Nathaniel. She wants me to bring him into the office sometime, but I don't know about that. I don't know if people are ready for it. And I don't need creeps like Gene and Rochelle and Lynn—who's in no position to talk—staring at my poor little baby and thinking he's a freak.

And thinking I deserved it. Oh, I'm not exaggerating. I could hear it in Frieda's voice when she called. Like she was happy something went wrong. I mean, she ain't cruel or nothing, I ain't saying that. But I can tell it somehow made her feel better. But Ange was never one to take no pleasure in other people's aggravation.

I don't wanna stay on too long with Ange 'cause I wanna catch a nap while Natey's sleeping. Kath is coming by later and she'll watch him while I go out and take a walk if I can manage it. Maybe go into a store. I guess it's pretty much all over the neighborhood by now and I'm gonna have to face people.

It's funny, too. I mean, when I decided to go ahead and have the kid on my own, I couldn't be bothered about what people thought. But now, I don't wanna see nobody. I can't face nobody. I mean, all the doctors tell me I didn't do nothing wrong. So what is it? I'm busy thinking about this and hardly even listening to Ange.

"You'll never guess who's leaving!" she's saying.

"Huh? Who?"

"Yoshi."

"Really? He just got there."

"I know. Guys like that, they don't stay around too long."

"Hey, Yoshi's not so bad."

"I guess your friend Fern would know about that."

It's hopeless. She'll never change.

"So what about you, Ange?"

"Oh, we're doing great." She sounds real cheery. "Jim's taking it pretty good. Real quiet. Sometimes he gets these shakes in his legs, and that gets him real mad. Curses like a sailor. But other than that, he don't say much."

"You, uh, never talk about what happened?"

"Oh, Tina, what good would that accomplish? You know, sometimes it's better to leave things alone."

"I guess, Ange."

"I mean, I got my hands full taking care of him the way it is."

"Don't it bother you having to take care of him? I mean, after everything that happened and all."

"Jesus, Tina, what kind of question is that? The poor man's my husband."

"Sure, Ange, I know."

She drops it.

"It'll be great when you come back, Tina. I miss you."

"I know, kiddo. I know you can't go to the bathroom by yourself."

"Yeah, I'm afraid I'll get trapped in there by Rochelle."

"Tell me about it."

But I'm thinking, I don't really wanna go back. It's like, that part of my life is ended. It would be spooky to go back, like going through a time warp. Like entering the past in one of them "Twilight Zone" episodes. I gotta move on. I'm thinking maybe I'll take one of them two-year degrees at some fashion school like FIT or the Laboratory Institute of Merchandising I heard some of the people at *Skirt* talking about. I mean, I could really do something with that.

"I don't know, Ange. Maybe I could come back but get a job at *Skirt* or *Table and Chairs* or something instead," I says to her.

"Oh come on, Tina, they're a bunch of weirdos. All those faggoty guys."

"Don't say that, Ange. I mean, they're different and all. But I think I'd like working there."

I can tell she's hurt. "Well, you didn't used to think so. But I guess you got a lot on your mind right now."

"Yeah, I guess."

She waits a minute then aks, "So what about this guy?"

"What guy?"

"'What guy?' she says. "The lawyer guy."

"You mean Noah?"

"Yeah. That his name?"

"Yeah."

"So you gonna marry him?"

"I don't know, Ange. I never felt like this about nobody before. But I don't think it's gonna work. I mean, Noah's the kind of guy, the minute he sees what he wants, he's not so sure he wants it anymore."

I don't think she understands what I'm getting at. "Hey," she says, "that don't mean nothing. Use the right approach, a woman can make a guy do anything. You just gotta push a little, is all. He'll come around."

"I don't know, Ange. There's more to it than that."

"Listen to me, Tina. You can have anybody you want."

She can't look at it no other way. How can she still be dealing in dreams? But I can't fool myself I don't think all the time about marrying Noah. Shit, I already got the dress. But all I say is, "I can't worry about that now. I gotta take care of Natey."

"Oh, Tina."

"You know what gets me crazy? Them poking at him all the time. Sometimes I just don't wanna take him to no more doctors."

"Oh, but, Tina, they're always making advances. Maybe they'll find a cure or something."

"Ange, it ain't like that. It ain't like you can take a pill or something and make it better."

She don't say nothing. I notice people shut up pretty quick when you tell 'em there's not too much can be done. They don't know what to say. No one wants to hear yeah, it's horrible, and it's always gonna be that way.

"Ange," I says, "I gotta face facts. I'm gonna fight any bastard ever says a mean thing about my kid. But I got a baby with a deformed arm. That's the way it is." ·

"Oh, Tina. You're taking it pretty good. Not everybody could take it the way you do."

Then I'm crying. 'Cause I'm the biggest phony ever lived. Yeah I'm taking it so well. My poor little baby.

"Ange, Ange. It's so ugly. Oh, Ange. I hate it so much."

Chapter 48

Shit. He's up again. The kid can't sleep. Every time I lie down or try to eat something or maybe read for a minute he wakes up. I mean, I can hardly drag myself around, but I also kind of like getting up with him and holding him, like no two people was ever that close. In the middle of the night like this, I feel it's just the two of us in our own little world.

He's smart, too. He can hear the cars go by. He kind of perks up and listens. Of course, around here, you don't get too many cars at three o'clock in the morning. I don't know. Maybe he can't sleep 'cause he's upset. Although probably he's too young to know what's going on.

I was dreaming about Ma. Like I went in to get Natey from the crib, except I forgot I had Natey exactly, you know? And when I reached down, Ma was there, all small and thin, and I held her.

I sent Ma a picture with the baby kind of covered up. I figure, why get into it? I don't know what she can take. Some of the people at her place sent me some stuff they made for Natey. These sad little crocheted poodles made from shiny orange, brown, and white yarn. I stuck them in a drawer. Maybe it's mean or stupid or something, but I just don't want them around.

I guess I should feel lucky so far they didn't find too much else wrong with him. Just something in his urinary tract they can fix. Still. I don't feel fucking lucky. What gets me is that here I have this baby, and instead of people talking about how cute he is and how big he's getting or how he's eating or what he's doing, everybody's talking about his arm and the doctors. Like I've got this condition instead of a kid.

I aksed Fern to get me a book on orthopedics so's I could learn all the names for everything. And I got everybody to aks around for who's a good doctor to see. There's a guy Chanson up at the Presbyterian supposed to be the best.

I bought myself one of them datebooks or organizers or whatever it is you call 'em. Just to keep the doctors' appointments straight. Not to mention flying up to Childrens in Boston. Only thing I don't like is when they have these other doctors there and it's like a show 'cause we're this interesting case. Like those demonstrations for gadgets they do in stores. "Here, doctor, maybe you can learn something from this. You don't see this every day." Like they don't notice that the arm is attached to a baby. But some of them are real nice. Like they're sad about it. Like they're people, too.

It's hard sometimes watching the TV or even hearing people talk, 'cause all I hear is the word "arm" or "hand" jumping out at me like someone was shouting. Or I find myself staring at people's arms and hands, especially kids'. Like the whole fucking rest of the world is normal.

Boy, I really fucked up this time. I always think I know what I'm doing. No one can tell me shit. I was so smart, I wanted a baby. Well, I got myself a baby. Joke's on me. I bet that's what they're all saying.

People probably think I feel guilty about what happened, but that's not even it. It's like, when there's something wrong, it don't just disappear. I always knew there was this sickness somewhere in me, something different, wrong, inside, and now it's on the outside. I should of known, but I was too dumb to see it coming. Sometimes I think I'm too stupid to live.

And what makes it even worse is Jeannie staying away. Sometimes you can't plug up a hole no matter how much you put in it. I mean, without Jeannie to turn to, Kathy and Pop and Fern and Ange and Noah put together ain't enough. I guess that's 'cause when we was kids I always had her there. Maybe it was too hard on her, being the older one. I mean, I had her, but what did she have? Maybe she felt what was missing more than I did. There was always something missing with this family. And now Natey's arm not quite there.

I don't even know how much Jeanette knows about Natey, 'cause she always changes the subject or it's like she's not listening or something. The way she is, I can't even talk to her about it 'cause she don't wanna hear. Like she's pretending nothing happened. It sucks. Maybe you miss some of the bad stuff that way, but you miss a whole hell of a lot else, too. I don't know, maybe she'll come to his high school graduation.

Fern thinks maybe I should talk to her shrink or something. Like I don't know what the matter is. "So why are you depressed, Ms. Scacciapensieri? Oh. You have a baby with a horribly deformed arm? Oh. I get it."

I don't wanna talk to nobody. I don't need nobody trying to cheer me up and that shit. I mean, this is the way it's gonna be for the rest of my life, the rest of *his* life, and the sooner everybody gets used to it, the better. I mean, it's easy for them, ain't it? They don't gotta live with it. They don't gotta fucking face the stupid goddamn neighbors with their pitying smiles. Or the ones afraid to look. Oh, they think I don't see them? The jerks.

I tell you, I'm sick of all of 'em. Yeah, Noah with his fucking handouts, and even Kathy running over here to babysit or coming with me to the doctors like she's trying to make up for something. I guess it's better than going by myself, although I don't know what she's getting out of it 'cause they never say nothing new. Then she's gotta tell Pop. The two of them can cry on each other's shoulders. And I was liking her and all, but how can she help me now? There's things in this world no one can help with.

I mean, even Ange don't have it so bad, right?

Chapter 49

Pop says every time I got a doctor's appointment to take a cab, but I like the subway. Really. I mean, I put Natey in the Snugli and no one can tell practically there's anything wrong. I mean, you take a cab, it's like it's this big deal or something. Not to mention the money. Although Pop keeps saying he'll pay for it. "Take a cab," he tells me. "It's nicer."

Kath is trying to be all sweet and she says she don't care how we go, even though today we gotta switch trains and go all the hell the way uptown to Babies.

The F ain't too bad, not too crowded or dirty, and I'm sitting like a bump not saying a word to Kath, just looking up at the advertisements. There's one for toilet paper with some intellectual-type guy telling you in Spanish about how great the stuff is. Then another for a bug spray. It shows this lady all put out 'cause roaches crawled over her baked chicken in front of company. Jesus. And right next to it they got an ad for an airline. Palm trees and sun and the ocean. Get away from it all. You know what I mean. I guess who's ever paying for these things, they're not real sure who their audience is.

Then there's one for some tea, the steam rising from a giant cup. It makes me think about the red-and-gold tin like a little pirate's treasure chest Grandma always used to keep in the house. Sweet something. Swee-Touch-Nee. Poor old Grandma.

We get out at Jay Street and wait for the A. Kathy's going on about something but I ain't listening, so she goes to the newsstand to buy a paper to kill some time, 'cause it looks like this train ain't never gonna come, who knows what the problem is, they ain't gonna tell you.

> *I'm a little teapot, short and stout.*
> *Here is my handle, here is my spout.*
> *I can change my handle for my spout.*
> *Just tip me over, pour me out.*

And suddenly I'm thinking I gotta get away. I don't want this baby, this broken baby, like Donna said. I can take the subway to Penn Station and then grab a train for someplace. Just untie the fucking Snugli and leave the baby on the platform, although it's a bitch to take the thing off.

Then I realize that's crazy and I'd have to go home first, get some cash, maybe fly somewhere instead. Anyplace is okay, L.A. or something like that like they showed in that ad. Someplace clean and sunny.

I heard of people doing that. Starting over fresh. I could change my name. People do it in the movies all the time. Like when they're in some kind of trouble, the law or whatever, but really they're innocent or maybe what they did wasn't so bad anyways. Or when some maniac is after them. They pick up and go. New York ain't the only fucking place in the world. People live other places, too, and I bet it's almost as good. I could do it. I could even go to fucking Europe if I got a passport. I would love that. Someplace where they even speak different and I'd have to learn. Italy, like goddamn Noah went to. And maybe after they all calmed down and stopped looking for me I'd send them all a fucking postcard.

I could have a beautiful life if I'd just move myself to do something about it. When you're stuck in a mess you don't just gotta stay there and sink. Like some people, they have problems, all's they can think of is to kill themselves. Plenty of 'em have done it right down here too, jumped right onto the tracks.

So I'm looking down and thinking how ever since you're a kid they're warning you: "Don't stand too near the tracks! Stay away from the third rail!" And I realize I don't know which one is the fucking third rail. Can you believe it? My whole fucking life in this city and I don't know what the fucking third rail looks like. What a little dope. So I'm thinking maybe I should aks somebody but that just seems too stupid for words. Anyways, I guess those people commit suicide figured it out. And let's say they jumped and missed the third rail. The train would come along and crush them, right? So one way or the other it don't matter. Except that I'd like to know.

I guess it makes a real mess. I mean, they gotta shut down the train and everybody gets pissed. They all gotta take Sixth Avenue service. It could back things up for hours. People'd be cursing, not knowing what the fuck was going on and being late for everything. Stamping their feet and muttering, "Goddamn trains."

But when they got home and read about it in the *Post* or something, they feel real bad maybe. Think the person was nuts for knocking themselves off whatever the trouble. "Had to be. Hell, there are worse things."

Natey's crying a little so I walk around rocking him and I get him quiet again. It's easy with him so close to me in the Snugli anyways, like he's still inside of me, like we're one person. If I did leave, what would happen to him? I mean, should I just hand him off to Kath first? She'd wanna keep him and all, I guess, but what about Pop?

Maybe it's not such a good idea, 'cause how the hell will Nate feel his mother skipped out 'cause she couldn't stand it? I mean, that's not exactly the message I wanna start him out with. And would Kathy keep all the appointments and stay with him in the hospital and hold him at night when he can't get to sleep? And probably it would get everyone real upset, even Noah, not to mention everybody else, including Jeanette and Ma.

I head down towards the newsstand 'cause I'm getting nervous Kathy's taking so long. I notice all the people. In the middle of the day, too. I mean, what are they all doing here? It's like, when you're working, you think everybody else is working, too. Nine to five. But when you're home, it's like you see this whole other part of the world. All this life going on outside the office window. Sometimes I feel I'll live in New York a hundred years and never see the half of it.

Of course, they could clean this place up a bit. I mean, the smell, the candy wrappers. Not exactly cheery. Must be pretty goddamn depressing to work down here all day. Those guys must go a little crazy.

So here comes Kath and I see what's taking her so long. She's got *Parenting* and *Woman's Day* and *Family Circle* and *Working Woman*, all this stuff about kids and decorating and clothes and careers, just things she thinks I'd like, and then the train's here and we grab seats and flip open the magazines and look through them making comments and laughing and pointing stuff out to each other and the trip goes along like nothing; we'll be there before we even notice, we're so busy talking.

DELIGHT IN THE NOVELS
OF AWARD-WINNING

SHELBY HEARON

☐ A SMALL TOWN
(A39-261, $9.95, USA)($12.95, Can)
"An evocative and sweetly charming story about disappearing
America...Decorated with rich detail, full of comedy...
refreshingly straightforward, A SMALL TOWN is a large
success." —*Boston Herald*

☐ OWNING JOLENE
(A35-744, $4.95, USA)($5.95, Can)
"Refreshing irreverent...crisp prose spiked with wit and earthy
Texas imagery...The book belongs to Jolene, whose coming of
age won't remind you of anyone else's." —*Los Angeles Times*

☐ GROUP THERAPY
(A36-063, $4.95, USA)($5.95, Can)
"Fresh and comic...deals with the differences between North
and South, black and white, adults and teenagers, but
especially between women and men." —*People*

Ⓦ Warner Books P.O. Box 690
New York, NY 10019

Please send me the books I have checked. I enclose a check or money
order (not cash), plus 95¢ per order and 95¢ per copy to cover postage
and handling,* or bill my ☐ American Express ☐ VISA ☐ MasterCard.
(Allow 4-6 weeks for delivery.)

___Please send me your free mail order catalog. (If ordering only the
catalog, include a large self-addressed, stamped envelope.)

Card # _____

Signature _____ Exp. Date _____

Name _____

Address _____

City _____ State _____ Zip _____
*New York and California residents add applicable sales tax.   529